104

She had no desire to fight him

Garrick's quizzical glance met hers with a hint of amusement. "Aren't you going to struggle?"

"If I did," Kim replied, "it might only encourage you."

"You could always try that well-worn line about not being that kind of girl."

"I don't think I'm the kind of girl you had in mind when you said that," she retorted.

Garrick's brows rose mockingly. "At least you're very self-possessed! If I'd made any impression, shouldn't you be trembling in my arms?"

"So far you've done nothing to make me," Kim replied lightly, hoping he didn't notice her racing pulse. She had no great faith in the self-possession he spoke of.

"So the fault is mine?" he said lazily, pulling her closer as he slowly lowered his mouth to kiss her soft lips.

D1010213

MARGARET PARGETER

is also the author of these

Harlequin Presents

145—STORMY RAPTURE
366—SAVAGE POSSESSION
431—THE DARK OASIS
453—BOOMERANG BRIDE
503—COLLISION
523—THE LOVING SLAVE
540—NOT FAR ENOUGH
548—STORM CYCLE
572—PRELUDE TO A SONG
580—SUBSTITUTE BRIDE
588—CLOUDED RAPTURE

and these

Harlequin Romances

2211—THE JEWELLED CAFTAN
2227—THE WILD ROWAN
2241—A MAN CALLED CAMERON
2260—MARRIAGE IMPOSSIBLE
2284—ONLY YOU
2296—THE DEVIL'S BRIDE
2350—AUTUMN SONG
2375—KISS OF A TYRANT
2409—DARK SURRENDER
2416—DECEPTION
2422—CAPTIVITY
2475—AT FIRST GLANCE

Many of these books are available at your local bookseller.

For a free catalog listing all titles currently available,
send your name and address to:

HARLEQUIN READER SERVICE
1440 South Priest Drive, Tempe, AZ 85281
Canadian address: Stratford, Ontario N5A 6W2

MARGARET PARGETER

man from the kimberleys

Harlequin Books

TORONTO • NEW YORK • LOS ANGELES • LONDON
AMSTERDAM • PARIS • SYDNEY • HAMBURG
STOCKHOLM • ATHENS • TOKYO • MILAN

Harlequin Presents first edition May 1983
ISBN 0-373-10595-9

Original hardcover edition published in 1982
by Mills & Boon Limited

Copyright © 1982 by Margaret Pargeter. All rights reserved.
Philippine copyright 1982. Australian copyright 1982.
Cover illustration copyright © 1983 by Tom Bjarnason Inc.
Except for use in any review, the reproduction or utilization of
this work in whole or in part in any form by any electronic,
mechanical or other means, now known or hereafter invented,
including xerography, photocopying and recording, or in any
information storage or retrieval system, is forbidden without
the permission of the publisher, Harlequin Enterprises Limited,
225 Duncan Mill Road, Don Mills, Ontario, Canada M3B 3K9.

All the characters in this book have no existence outside the
imagination of the author and have no relation whatsoever to
anyone bearing the same name or names. They are not even
distantly inspired by any individual known or unknown to the
author, and all the incidents are pure invention.

The Harlequin trademarks, consisting of the words
HARLEQUIN PRESENTS and the portrayal of a Harlequin,
are trademarks of Harlequin Enterprises Limited and are registered
in the Canada Trade Marks Office; the portrayal of a Harlequin is
registered in the United States Patent and Trademark Office.

Printed in U.S.A.

CHAPTER ONE

IT was hot waiting at the International Airport in Perth, Australia. Kim Grantley rubbed a clammy hand over her equally sticky brow as she gazed around. The airport was pleasant, with its Western Australian flowers and shrubs, but she felt too tired and anxious to appreciate it. She hoped her uncle Joe, with whom she was going to stay, wouldn't be long in coming to collect her. It might have been easier if she had known what he looked like, but her parents only had one photograph of him, taken on his wedding day, thirty years ago, and he must have changed from the rather stocky young man he had been then.

In the heat Kim's eyes closed gently, her usual vitality drained by the excitement and drama of the long plane journey from England. Yet she had no feeling of being in a strange land. In fact, she had an incredible sense of homecoming which she couldn't account for. It was crazy, she mused, an odd smile playing gently on her soft mouth. England was her home and she would be returning there in six months' time, at the most, if all went well.

Someone pushed against her and, as her eyes flew open, she noticed a tall, dark man standing staring at her, about ten yards away.

Kim frowned. The man's head was set at an arrogant angle. As she stared back his brows rose and his mouth tightened to a decisive line. Ignoring her cool, keep-your-distance expression, he approached, his lips curving suddenly with a hint of amusement.

In two seconds, long swinging strides brought his big, powerful body directly in front of her. 'Do you by any chance happen to be Miss Kim Grantley?' he asked.

5

Kim's beautiful violet blue eyes widened as she was pinned to the spot by the steady gaze of light grey ones. His direct glance and deep voice, with only the slightest intonation to suggest he was Australian, sent a peculiar shiver right through her.

'Yes,' she heard herself mumbling stupidly, 'I think I am.'

'You'd better be sure!' This time he actually laughed at her. 'I can't go back with the wrong girl.'

Aware that she must sound foolish, Kim sought to hide her embarrassment. 'I don't know who you are,' she stammered, 'but I'm sure you can't be my uncle.'

'I hope not,' he murmured sardonically. 'Who would want to be the uncle of such a lovely young lady?'

Kim's glance unconsciously sharpened. In front of her, she felt sure, was a man with a great deal of experience when it came to women and not one to resort to rather obvious compliments. Somehow she knew that whether he considered her lovely or not, it wouldn't bother him a bit if he were never to see her again.

A little stung, because she was instinctively sure this was true, she said coldly, 'As I'm not a mind-reader it might be a good idea if you introduced yourself. I don't think you're the kind of man who would need to haunt a place like this in order to find himself some feminine company.'

'Indeed not,' he replied softly, with just enough steel in his voice to warn her to be careful of what she said.

His arrogance irritated her even more when she realised it wasn't out of place, allied as it was to his undoubted good looks. All the same, she was sure a good set-down would do him no harm. She couldn't imagine herself as being the one to administer it, though.

'So,' she strove to stay calm beneath his continuing regard, 'who are you?'

Deviously he replied, 'Your uncle Joe asked me to meet you.'

Momentarily diverted she exclaimed, 'Why couldn't he have come himself?'

He shrugged broad shoulders. 'Your aunt isn't well. Nothing to get alarmed about,' he assured her quickly. 'He just didn't want to leave her, and I was coming in in any case.'

The apprehension in Kim's eyes turned to bewilderment. 'There's my cousin, though.' A gasp suddenly escaped her. 'You don't happen to be my cousin, by any chance?'

'Your cousin is only twenty-six,' he drawled. 'Didn't you know?'

'Yes.' She flushed, reluctant to confess that Brian's age was almost all she did know about him.

'I can give him ten years,' the man smiled. 'I'm not sure whether to be annoyed or flattered?'

'By my mistake, you mean?' she retorted. 'I wasn't thinking, that's all, and I've no idea what my cousin looks like. But,' she stared resentfully at him, 'it might simplify matters if you could bring yourself to tell me who you are, unless we're to stand here all day.'

'You are in a hurry,' he teased.

'I don't think so,' because she was tired, she failed to control a flash of anger, 'but if everyone in this country is in as great a hurry as you are, it's a wonder you get anything done at all!'

His lazy indolence was merely a smoke screen. She saw this as his eyes cooled frostily. Too late she realised that here was a man who worked at high pressure, who could move with incredible speed, should he choose to do so. And give orders at the same rate!

'If you intend enjoying your holiday,' he snapped, 'I shouldn't go round expressing too many views like that.'

'I'm sorry,' she whispered, aghast that she could have said such a thing. 'You're right, of course. It was unforgivable of me.'

His stern face relaxed again and he held out his hand. 'I'm sorry too,' he apologised. 'You were so suspicious but I shouldn't have let it provoke me. Otherwise, young lady,' he smiled wryly, 'you'd have known who I was immediately and we'd have been out of here by now. I'm Garrick Lang—your uncle works for me.'

Kim's smaller hand was swallowed up in his and the contact seared her. When he dropped her hand quickly she wondered if he had felt the same discomfort. She was relieved when he said curtly, 'We'd better be getting on our way, Miss Grantley, unless you want to attract the attention of one of our more enterprising photographers.'

'Who? Me?' Now he wasn't touching her she dared relax. 'Why should I?'

'Why shouldn't you?' Picking up her luggage, he shot her a slanting glance. 'U.K. visitors are always news, and you're more eye-catching than most. Even with that baby silk plait hanging down your back making you look about sixteen.'

'I'm four years older.'

'So Joe told me.'

As she followed Garrick Lang, she wondered what else her uncle had told him. 'Yet you had trouble spotting me?' she frowned.

'It wasn't easy,' he admitted. 'It might have helped if Joe had had a photograph.'

'Oh, but,' she paused, 'I thought . . .'

'Yes?' Garrick Lang murmured softly.

'Oh, nothing,' she nearly stumbled. She was sure her mother had sent a photograph about two months ago. Yes—hadn't Aunt Rose mentioned it in her last letter? She had said Joe was delighted to see how pretty Kim had grown. It was strange they hadn't shown it to Garrick Lang. Endeavouring to change the subject, she asked quickly, 'What time do we get to Coolarie? Do you live there as well?'

'Usually,' he replied levelly. 'And we'll be there late tomorrow.'

'Not until then?' He was hustling her through formalities, hailing a cab, but she scarcely noticed. 'I didn't know it was that far.'

'It isn't, Miss Grantley.' He studied her startled face as they settled in the taxi. 'To you it might seem so, but we can be there in a few hours. Unfortunately the business I had to attend to is taking longer than I expected. I have to see someone in the morning, so our departure has had to be postponed.'

Her wide violet eyes fixed on him in dismay. 'Won't they be wondering where I am? Won't Aunt Rose be worried?'

'I've been in touch and explained.' His manner suggested it was good of him to have spared the time.

Kim bristled at his extreme high-handedness, but she merely said in a low voice, 'I wish you hadn't. I could easily have gone on alone.'

Sadly he shook his head. 'Didn't it ever occur to you to study a map of Australia before you came here?'

'Of course I did!' she retorted indignantly. 'I do realise it's a big country, but I also know you have roads and public transport, and a girl might be as safe here as anywhere, travelling on her own.'

'It's a thousand miles,' he said softly, 'to Coolarie, and although we have roads, no public transport comes anywhere near the station. As you haven't a car, how would you propose getting there?'

'I'm afraid I didn't understand.' Flushing, she looked away from him uncomfortably. 'Uncle Joe said he would meet me and take me straight home. I'm sorry if I seemed silly—I expect it's because I'm feeling disappointed.'

'Never mind,' Garrick Lang smiled magnanimously. 'What's a little setback at your age? And I can almost guarantee you'll enjoy this one. And, after a good night's rest, you'll probably feel more able to meet your relations?'

'Where are we going?' she asked suddenly as they

sped through wide, busy streets. She didn't recognise any place—but then she didn't expect to.

'One of the city's best hotels. I wouldn't want you to leave with a bad impression.'

One of the city's best hotels! It sounded terribly expensive. Still, she might manage one night. She'd rather die than let this big, arrogant Aussie think she couldn't afford it. Uncle Joe had sent her air tickets and made sure she understood this was to be a free holiday, and if Coolarie was as isolated as Garrick Lang seemed to suggest, there might not be a lot to spend money on. What little she had might go a long way.

'Stop worrying,' he commanded gently, almost as if he had read her thoughts. 'The delay is my fault and your accommodation will be on me. If you're worrying about being in my debt,' he added smoothly, as she gazed at him uncertainly, 'don't. If you feel it necessary, I'm sure you'll find some way of repaying me at Coolarie.'

As his glance lingered on her she stirred uneasily, wishing he would look elsewhere. She wasn't to know how the sheer beauty of her face caught and held his attention. Her thick gilt hair, shimmering like silk in the sunlight, framed perfect features covered by clean, blemish-free skin. Her eyes were wide and blue, her nose straight, her mouth soft and passionate—too much so, the man considered, to be as innocent as it looked.

With a harshly drawn sigh, as her discomfort grew, he averted his gaze. 'How many boy-friends have you left behind?' he asked abruptly.

'No one special,' she flushed slightly, 'but would it matter if I had? Uncle Joe wanted to know the same thing.'

'Did he now?' Garrick Lang's hard jaw tightened. 'How interesting!'

'I don't think he was merely being curious,' she defended her uncle quickly. 'He did ask me to stay six months, so I suppose he wouldn't want me to decide there was someone I couldn't wait to get home to as soon as I arrived. After all,' her flush deepened, as she forced herself to confess honestly, 'he did pay for my ticket.'

'I see.' Again there was the oddly narrowed glance which she didn't understand.

Quickly she looked away, finding it easier to concentrate on the passing scenery. At least it didn't stare back at her, contemplating her with eyes which betrayed little while missing nothing. She felt herself go hot and swallowed several times. He affected her self-possession. With all her heart she wished her aunt and uncle had come to meet her themselves—or sent her cousin.

'Does my cousin work for you, too?' she asked suddenly. 'My uncle seems to think a lot of him.'

'He works for me when he's around,' Garrick Lang replied briefly.

Something in his voice returned Kim's eyes to his face, but again she could read little from his expression. His gaze was still perceptive, but otherwise an inscrutable mask. With a sigh she turned back to the window. Had Brian displeased him? she wondered. When Garrick Lang spoke of him there was something in his voice which seemed to suggest Brian didn't warrant his full approval.

Owning that it might be wiser to wait until she got to Coolarie before jumping to too many conclusions, she lapsed into silence, and was relieved when they drew up almost immediately outside a hotel. Her relief was short-lived when she saw that it was even more luxurious than she had feared, but she made no protest. If Garrick Lang had decided they should stay here there was nothing she could do, but she would insist on paying for her own room.

Inside, after he had checked in at the desk, they were duly shown to their rooms on the first floor. 'I'm just along the corridor, should you want me,' Garrick said as they paused outside her door. When she thanked him shyly, he advised in clipped tones, 'You look exhausted. I should have a shower and rest, if I were you. I'll call for you in a couple of hours' time for dinner.'

After he had gone she was possessed by a strange restlessness which she realised must be over-excitement and travel fatigue, the jet lag which long-distance travellers were warned about. 'It will take you days to get over it,' a family friend had said.

Would it? On the whole, Kim was sure she didn't feel too bad. Impatiently she suspected the peculiar tension she felt had as much to do with Garrick Lang as the long journey she had just completed. When he looked at her, her nerves seemed to dance and her heart beat faster. He was very attractive, she'd have to be blind not to see that, but so were a lot of men. So why was he having this devastating effect on her? Kim frowned at such an extravagant expression, yet couldn't altogether dismiss it. She was forced to amend her former thoughts. There might be a lot of men like Garrick Lang, but, if there were, she'd never met them. Working in the shop, as she did when she was at home, she was in constant contact with many men, but until now none of them had ever stirred her imagination. She remembered asking her mother, once, if her apparent immunity was unnatural, and her mother had merely laughed and shaken her head.

'You're young—give yourself time,' she had replied. 'One of these days you'll meet someone and fall in love. It happens to us all, eventually.'

Sighing, Kim turned to her suitcase, searching for her bathrobe and hairbrush. She was certain she wasn't falling in love with Garrick Lang, but whatever it was that she felt, it was extremely uncomfortable!

Later, bathed, rested and dressed again, she was ready when he knocked. It was the kind of hotel where she guessed one might be expected to dress for dinner, but she had compromised by wearing a silky two-piece, the full skirt sweeping just below her knees. A wide satin sash narrowed her small waist down to nothing while a matching band of ribbon restricted her now loosened hair. She had smoothed the merest film of foundation over her pale skin, and accentuated her vulnerable mouth with a soft pink lipstick. Hoping, like a meal, she was neither over or underdone, she went anxiously to open the door.

Her nervousness was reflected in her smile as Garrick Lang's glance flickered over her and a somewhat reluctant glint of admiration appeared in the depth of his grey eyes. Slowly they explored her budding young curves, the slender, graceful lines of her young body. Then the grey of his eyes was half hidden by narrowed lids and he merely murmured coolly between tightening lips, 'You look charming, Miss Grantley.'

Her smile fading before such cool formality, she managed to say thank you. Then, making an effort to dissolve the frost in his face, she tried again. 'Please, won't you call me Kim?'

'I'd be delighted to,' his mouth relaxed, teasingly, 'if you'll agree to drop the Mr Lang.'

'Oh, yes—Garrick.' To her chagrin she flushed as she was unable to resist the temptation of allowing his name to roll experimentally off the end of her tongue. Quickly, trying to rectify her mistake, she flustered, 'You didn't have to offer, you know. I mean, I wasn't angling.' Beginning to feel a complete fool, she rushed on breathlessly, 'What I'm trying to say is that, as you're my uncle's employer . . .'

As her voice trailed off helplessly, he merely smiled, drawing her out of the room and closing the door. Before she was quite aware of it happening, he had whisked her downstairs and to the bar. Placing two hands around her waist, he lifted her, before she could protest, on to a bar-stool. As though the break in their conversation had never occurred, he drawled, 'Your uncle also happens to be my late father's second cousin, which makes him a distant relation. So, circumstances being what they are, I think we might dispense with formality a little sooner than we might otherwise have done.'

Dazedly, Kim nodded, still feeling his hands on her waist, his cool, clean breath on her face. 'Whatever you say,' she whispered.

Smilingly he teased, as he ordered two drinks, 'Get that line off by heart and I'm sure to enjoy your visit!'

Kim breathed a sigh of relief that he was being so nice, but she wished her treacherous heart would stop beating so enthusiastically. Niceness to Garrick Lang would only mean politeness, the usual courtesy he would normally extend to any guest. And, she supposed, for this one night, anyway, this was what she was. Glancing sideways, she was intensely conscious of the nearness of him, of how attractive he looked in a dark blue suit. He was a big man, powerful and assured, yet she had a startling urge to run her fingers through his short, crisply curling dark hair. Even her body seemed to be reaching out to him and, despite a twinge of nervous fear, she felt excited. He had a kind of animal magnetism which drew her as surely as she tried to resist it. Shivering, she wondered if she could possibly be falling in love.

Suddenly, realising she was staring, she dropped her thick lashes. With an effort she reminded herself that she had only known him a few hours. Her voice, when she spoke, was quite two notes higher than usual; she had to pause and begin again. 'I remember Daddy saying Uncle Joe was related to the man he worked for, but he thought the relationship was very distant.' She hesitated, toying nervously with the glass of sherry he set before her. 'I'm afraid, over the years, our two families haven't had much to do with each other.'

Garrick Lang shrugged easily. 'Your father, I believe, didn't approve of his sister marrying Joe.'

'No—well,' Kim hesitated uncertainly, 'from what I gather it was my grandparents who weren't very pleased, but I suppose that was understandable. Australia is on the other side of the world, and thirty years ago it probably seemed a lot farther.' When Garrick made no comment, she added hurriedly, 'Aunt Rose is almost ten years older than my father. I think he was only about twenty when it happened.'

'Yet old enough to side with your grandparents.'

'Perhaps,' Kim agreed awkwardly, then, with a rueful grin, 'I might have answered your question better if I'd been there at the time, but I wasn't. Mummy once told me it was because they were married so quickly, more than anything else. They'd only known each other a week.'

'So your father doesn't have anything against Joe specifically?'

'I know they didn't—well, hit it off.' She looked at Garrick Lang rather helplessly. 'I—I have heard him say he found my uncle too brash, but it—it's an opinion he seems to have of all Australians.'

Garrick grinned slightly. 'At least you're trying to be honest.'

'You asked me.'

'Yes, I did.' His mouth relaxed even more to allow a glint of white teeth. 'It's always interested me,' he mused, 'that none of your family has ever visited Rose.'

For all he spoke lightly, his tone implied they had been guilty of neglect. Kim considered this anxiously. Perhaps they had been? 'My grandparents aren't alive now,' she said slowly, 'but I think, when they were, they did make some attempt to bring about a reconciliation, shortly after Aunt Rose married. When they were both killed in an accident, two years later, Daddy wrote to Aunt Rose and since then they've always kept in touch, but unfortunately he's never had time to visit.'

'Why not?'

Disregarding Garrick's coolness, Kim did her best to try and explain. 'When my grandparents died, he had to leave university and take over the shop.'

'Shop?'

'Yes, hasn't Aunt Rose ever mentioned it?' As Garrick shook his head, she continued, 'Grandfather was an artist. In conjunction with that he ran an antique shop, just a small town affair, but Daddy was always very keen. To begin with, I believe, he had a struggle, but since then the business has expanded and he found it impossible to get away. Not long enough, anyway, to come all the way here.'

'Your mother, neither?'

'No, she helps him.'

'And you?'

'Yes, me too,' Kim nodded. 'Since I left school, nearly two years ago.'

'How are they managing without you now?' Garrick asked, watching her closely.

'Very well, I'm afraid,' Kim sighed, biting her lip unconsciously. 'You see, my twin brother and sister left school a few weeks ago. John's keen, so's Lucy, but it's not going to be possible for Daddy to employ all of us. The present recession isn't exactly helping the antique trade.'

Abstractedly, her eyes dwelt on the dark red sherry in her glass. When Uncle Joe had written, thanking her mother for her letter and the snapshots of Kim she had sent Rose, they had all been pleasantly surprised, as this was something he had never done before. Then he had surprised them again by asking if they could spare Kim for a long visit. Kim had been excited and keen to accept. The invitation, apart from anything else, might provide a way out of their immediate difficulties. After six months the unemployment situation might have eased, or Lucy might decide she'd rather go to college than stay in the shop.

'Why should you be the one to leave the nest?' she heard Garrick enquire.

'We don't have to leave, any of us,' she replied. 'It's really a case of economics, and I'm the eldest.'

'But you aren't trained for a career?'

Because she was inclined to secretly worry about the future, Kim tried to make a joke of it. Perversely she smiled. 'I'm very good at housekeeping. I spend a lot of time in the kitchen as Mummy prefers the shop, so, if all else fails, I might find something in that line.'

Garrick Lang didn't seem as amused as she had thought he might be. If anything his face darkened with what to Kim looked curiously like suspicion. 'You sound as if you might make some man an efficient wife. You might even settle here.'

'That's what Uncle Joe said,' Kim laughed, then flushed as again something in Garrick Lang's eyes made her uneasy. 'About staying—not getting married,' she exclaimed hastily.

When he didn't comment on this, she glanced at him anxiously. 'I'm really looking forward to meeting my new relations, especially Aunt Rose.'

This time Garrick condescended to speak. 'Rose is very nice, but very much under Joe's thumb.'

He sounded mild enough, as if it was something he was used to, so had she any reason for thinking he didn't approve of the situation? Kim's blue eyes shadowed with uncertainty. 'Perhaps she likes it that way? After all,' she jested ironically, 'a wife usually promises to obey.'

'Would you?' he asked mockingly.

For a long moment she considered, scarcely knowing why she was taking the conversation so seriously. 'If I trusted a man enough,' she said at last.

'What about love?' he jibed. 'Somehow I received the impression you'd be more romantic.'

'It pays to be practical,' she retorted, without any clear idea of what she meant. But wasn't it better that he should believe she was a girl able to control her emotions than one in danger of falling for the first Australian she had met?

Again he made no comment but maintained a rather grim silence. After finishing their drinks they went into dinner, Kim deciding he had lost interest in what they had been discussing. While they were eating, though, he encouraged her to talk of her life in England, and it wasn't until the meal was almost over that she suddenly realised he must have found out nearly everything about her.

Rather crossly, she made some attempt to redress the balance by asking about Coolarie. 'What does my uncle do, exactly?'

Garrick grinned derisively. 'Are you asking me?'

Kim was puzzled. 'Well, as my uncle's not here, I can't very well ask him!'

'His answer might be different from mine.'

'In what way?'

He shrugged, and Kim wished he wouldn't. It drew her attention to the breadth of his shoulders which immediately made her conscious of the obvious strength of his body. 'He might tell you he did all the work on the place?'

'And it wouldn't be true?'

'I don't think so.'

Impatiently, convinced Garrick Lang was playing some devious game of his own, Kim stirred a spoonful of sugar in her coffee. 'I'd like to hear your version.'

His mouth quirked. 'Joe book-keeps mostly—spends much of his time in the office where he feels at the hub of things. When I have to be away he likes to think he has complete control.'

'Are you away often?' Somehow she didn't feel so keen to talk about Joe.

Garrick studied her a moment before replying, and when he did she felt there was something deliberate about his answer. 'I have other properties, in Queensland and the Northern Territory, which I visit regularly, but I'm very fond of Coolarie. I was born there.'

'I see——' She hesitated. It was a rather odd situation. If Uncle Joe hadn't been a relation his exact position might have been clearer. As it was, she had no idea whether he was treated as one of the family or as a mere employee. Once at Coolarie it should be easy enough to discover for herself, and she thought she might be wiser to wait. She didn't dare risk possibly embarrassing Garrick Lang by being too persistent. Her uncle mightn't thank her for it! 'I didn't know,' she said, purposely keeping her voice light. 'Uncle Joe only told us that you lived with your mother and aren't married.'

Garrick looked hard at her, his grey eyes piercing and cool. 'I don't know why you are asking so many questions, when Joe appears to have told you everything that matters.'

Everything important, she almost said, and was thankful she had been able to stop such a confession escaping her lips. Garrick Lang was too astute and she would hate him to guess how she was beginning to feel about him. It was nothing she could put in words—how did one describe instant attraction without making it seem like something to joke about? But she was hollowly convinced that if he had been married she would have been dismayed.

After dinner she was sure he would tell her to have an early night or leave her to amuse herself. She was pleasantly surprised when he offered to take her for a quick tour of the area around the hotel. As she was still feeling refreshed by her rest earlier in the evening, she accepted with alacrity. She looked up at him and suddenly felt reassured. He was being friendly again, and when he was, as before, she found it impossible to resist him.

Outside the air was much fresher and cooler than it had been when they came in. Hearing her sigh of pleasure, Garrick smiled gently down on her.

'It's the wind. Local people sometimes call it the Fremantle doctor. In late afternoon and evening a sea breeze usually comes up the Swan River from the

Indian Ocean port of Fremantle and the temperature can drop in minutes.'

'The Swan River,' Kim said, 'has a nice sound.'

'It was so named,' Garrick explained, 'because of being the natural habitat of the black swan—beautiful birds, black with scarlet bills.'

The idea of swans being black amused Kim until it made her suddenly realise that a lot of things were going to be very different here from what they were at home. A bleak premonition, which she couldn't account for, stole over her and she shivered when she couldn't immediately throw it off. It could only be a touch of homesickness, she assured herself.

Garrick took her to Kings Park, a thousand-acre expanse of open ground near their hotel, within a mile of the city centre. Here there were wonderful, panoramic views of Perth and the water on which the city stood. The gardens, in early October, were glorious with wild flowers, startling Kim with their beauty.

'October is our spring,' Garrick reminded her, glancing with amusement at her incredulous face.

'When I go home I'll be all mixed up,' she laughed, not bothering to hide her amazement as she gazed her fill of the beautiful and varied landscape.

'It must be marvellous to have all this right in the middle of a city!'

'Perth's come a long way in recent years,' he said quietly. 'It's become very popular, but I still prefer the country.'

'Because you're a grazier?' Kim turned to look at him.

'Partly, I suppose,' he replied. 'I begin to feel stifled after even a few days in town.'

Kim didn't find this difficult to understand, although looking at him now, she thought he looked as much a successful business man as a grazier.

When she haltingly tried to tell him this, he smiled dryly. 'I have to be as much one as the other. In my grandfather's day, or even my father's, things were different, but, nowadays, I'm afraid the office claims a lot of my time. I'm in Sydney and Melbourne quite frequently, as well as Perth.'

He would appear to need his obvious vitality. While he was speaking she watched him closely, seeing the small lines etched around his eyes, the deeper ones around his strong mouth. These must be a sign that he was sometimes tired, and she didn't feel surprised.

'I'm glad we're going to Coolarie tomorrow,' she said softly, instinctively knowing he found even the mention of his home soothing.

Garrick nodded, his tone immediately brisker. 'It's always wonderful there—the wide plains, the deep gorges, the mountains. Nature in its most rugged form yet rewarding. You'll love it. You can see more of Perth on your way home.'

Strangely, she hated to be reminded she was only here for a little while. She heard herself saying rather sadly, 'Six months will soon pass.'

'It might not.'

Kim was surprised to feel threatened. Her eyes widened with a hint of alarm as she stared up at him. 'Somehow I don't think that was meant to be comforting, Mr Lang.'

'You noticed I said, might not?' He laid a hand on her shoulder while with his other he turned up her chin. 'It could be entirely up to you, remember that.'

She tried to free herself, but his grip merely tightened painfully. His long, steely fingers dug into her flesh and she winced. 'I don't think I understand you,' she gasped.

He snapped roughly, his hold on her absolute, 'Do you want to?'

Still feeling threatened, but as much by his closeness now as anything else, she breathed unevenly, 'I'm not sure.'

His mocking eyes correctly assessed her uncertainty. 'You feel as though you're standing on the edge of an abyss?'

When she whispered apprehensively, 'How did you guess?' some of the tension seemed to go out of him.

'You're very young,' he sighed tersely. 'You haven't learnt to hide your feelings properly, but it's important that you learn to stand on your own two feet. Don't let others manipulate you for their own gain—or what they imagine they might gain by it.'

'Why—why on earth should anyone want to do that?' Kim asked breathlessly, having not the faintest idea what he was talking about.

He shrugged lightly, then, as his anger dispersed, he chose to ignore her query. 'It might only be my imagination?' he drawled smoothly, letting go of her. 'Perhaps I've been working too hard lately. You'll just have to forgive me.'

CHAPTER TWO

THE air seemed to crackle with heat as they flew into Coolarie, late the following afternoon. Above her Kim saw a blue, cloudless sky, below the sprawling homestead of the cattle station. By her side sat Garrick Lang, flying the plane with a casual ease that told her, long before she asked, that he had flown for many years.

As he circled the landing-strip, prior to landing, he pointed out some figures down on the ground. 'Looks as if someone's waiting to welcome you,' he smiled.

'May I——' Kim hesitated, turning an excited face to him, 'I mean, do you think I might wave?'

'Go ahead.' His mouth quirked as his eyes met hers and lingered briefly before he brought the plane down expertly.

'That was wonderful!' she breathed, momentarily forgetting the reception committee, being overwhelmed by admiration. 'I scarcely felt a thing.'

'I should hope not!' He glanced at her again before swinging out of the plane and lifting her to the ground. For a moment his arms tightened as if he liked the feel of having her close to him. Then she was free. Taking no notice of the small gasp that escaped her as his hard grip left her strangely quivering, he turned to meet the man coming towards them. 'Here you are, Joe,' his hand snaked out to grasp Kim's wrist, drawing her forward, 'one charming niece, safely delivered.'

Joe Petre was still as short and stocky as Kim's father had described him, and, in his middle sixties, his face was lined, his hair grey. To Kim he was an elderly man, but one not wholly without distinction. About him was a certain neatness that appealed to her, and although his mouth and chin might have been weak, his face on the whole was pleasant.

Whether she approved of him or not, it seemed certain that he approved of her. 'I had no idea you were going to be so pretty!' he laughed, almost embarrassingly jubilant as he bestowed a smacking kiss on Kim's cheek. 'Your aunt will be delighted.'

Trying impatiently to banish the word brash from her mind, Kim freed her wrist from Garrick's hand and smiled back at him. She told herself she liked her uncle's enthusiasm. It wasn't fair that she should remember her father's opinion of him so vividly. In-laws were often inclined to be disparaging.

Joe talked to her a little longer before signalling to the young man standing a few yards behind him. 'Brian,' he beamed, 'come and meet your cousin from England.'

As the young man approached, Kim held out her hand. 'Hello,' she said rather nervously.

Brian stared at her moodily, his handshake so fleeting he scarcely touched her. He didn't speak, not until Garrick prompted coldly, 'Cat got your tongue, Brian?'

Brian flushed, then bowed with exaggerated politeness. 'Good afternoon, cousin,' he jeered. 'You may think I'm a fool, but you can see I'm wise enough to realise I must always obey the boss.'

Kim paled as she caught the rasp of Garrick's breath and saw his jaw tighten. But before she could say anything Joe, with a resigned glance at his son, intervened hastily.

'Your aunt didn't feel well enough to come and meet you, Kim. She started dinner, and I think that, and all the excitement, proved too much for her.'

'You must all have dinner at my house tonight, Joe,' Garrick said curtly.

Kim glanced at him unhappily, feeling the invitation might not have been given wholeheartedly. He must be tired and probably had no desire to entertain four extra people.

'I can help, Aunt Rose,' she began, only to be cut short by Joe's immediate acceptance.

'We'd be delighted, Garrick,' he smiled. 'I'm sure Kim will enjoy it.'

'You can count me out,' Brian muttered morosely.

'I was hoping I might be able to,' Garrick replied, no more politely, his tone grimly conveying his disapproval of the younger man.

There was a truck waiting, and Joe drove. Kim sat in the front between Garrick and her uncle while Brian slumped carelessly in the back. There wasn't much room, she was squashed up against Garrick and her skin seemed to burn. When, as if to give her some space, he dragged his arm out from between them to lay it along the back of her seat, she felt as disturbed as she might have been if he had held her in a close embrace.

As no one appeared to want to talk, she tried to concentrate on Brian's peculiar behaviour. Something was bothering him, and she wondered what it could be. He was quite good-looking and well dressed, but he didn't seem particularly content. It would have been easier if he'd even pretended to be pleased to see her. Kim bit her lip with an odd sense of frustration. Perhaps he would improve on acquaintance?

Joe stopped the truck in front of a large white house set in extensive gardens. Here Garrick Lang left them with a brief, 'See you later.' He didn't so much as spare Kim a glance as he reached for his light case and departed.

Joe's house, a few hundred yards away, wasn't nearly so big, but Kim was too eager to meet her aunt to bother about making comparisons. Rose Petre was a frail, rather tired-looking woman, a little younger than her husband. Once, Kim thought, she must have been very pretty.

As Joe had done, she smiled at Kim warmly. 'It's nice to see you, my dear,' she said. 'I'm so glad you were able to come.'

The sincerity of her welcome, and the fact that they immediately took to each other, made up a little for Brian's indifference. But though there were tears of happiness in Rose's eyes there was also doubt as she gazed at her brother's eldest child.

'You're a beautiful girl, but I didn't think you'd be so young!' she exclaimed, her manner somewhat confused as she let go of Kim and searched for her hankerchief.

Was her age so important? Why did something in her aunt's voice suggest it was? 'I'm twenty, Aunt Rose,' Kim murmured hesitantly.

'I know, my dear, but you don't look it,' Rose sighed.

'Mr Lang told me in Perth that you hadn't been well,' said Kim, after Rose had asked about her parents and the twins.

'That's true,' Rose admitted reluctantly. 'It's nothing really, though. I think, perhaps, what with one thing and another, I've just got a little run down.'

'I hope my visit won't be too much for you, then,' Kim replied anxiously. 'I'd hate to think I was making a lot of extra work.'

'Of course you won't be!' Joe boomed. 'You'll be as good as a tonic—won't she, love?' Placing an arm around his wife's drooping shoulders, he grinned happily, 'Take this evening, for instance. We've all been invited to dine with Garrick, so you won't have to cook, for a start.'

Rose frowned. 'His mother said nothing when I saw her this morning.'

'Garrick's just asked us, honey,' Joe assured her, with a quick wink at his wife which Kim felt instinctively she wasn't meant to see. It made her uneasy, especially as she noticed it deepened Rose's frown.

Rose appeared to make an effort to speak calmly. 'That will be nice, dear. Now,' she turned to Kim, 'we'll have a cup of tea, then I'll show you to your room. If we're going out later you'll want to freshen up.'

Joe said he would skip tea as he had some work to do. Brian had already disappeared. Kim would as soon have had fruit juice or just plain water, but as Rose had made the tea she didn't like to refuse. While they drank it Rose asked numerous questions about her brother and their relatives in England, all of which Kim did her best to answer satisfactorily.

'I'd better stop before I make us both quite home-sick!' Rose laughed gently, rising to her feet. 'Come on, I'll show you the rest of the house and then take you to your room.'

She wouldn't let Kim wash their teacups when she offered. 'You can help tomorrow,' she said.

Apart from the lounge there was a kitchen and dining-room and four bedrooms, the whole being neatly but sparsely furnished and all on one floor. 'One doesn't need a lot of furniture in such a hot climate,' Rose explained, as if apologising for the lack of it.

Kim thought of the oak beams and warm carpets, her mother's much loved antiques at home, and smiled ruefully. 'A lot of furniture can make a lot of extra work. When I think of all the hours I spend polishing . . .!'

It wasn't until she was alone in the small bedroom Rose gave her that she felt really curious about the bareness of her surroundings. Surely Uncle Joe, as Garrick's manager, must command a good salary? Idly she wondered what he spent it on. Obviously not his house!

After unpacking her luggage she had a shower and sat on her bed, as there wasn't a chair. She must remember to ask Aunt Rose if she could have one. She wasn't sure what to make of her relatives. They appeared to be a pleasant, ordinary enough family, so why did she feel there was a lot going on beneath the surface that she didn't yet know about? Then she reminded herself impatiently that no one was like an open book. They probably felt the same way about her.

Feeling, that at this stage, no useful purpose might be served by speculating about them, she allowed her thoughts to turn to Garrick Lang. What had he been trying to warn her of in Perth? And why had he decided against being more explicit? Of course he might merely have been going to point out, that because Aunt Rose wasn't very robust, she might be expected to do a lot for her. A man like Garrick Lang mightn't like the idea of anyone visiting his property and having to do a lot of work.

Thinking it was more than likely to be something like that, and not finding the prospect too daunting, she decided to wait and see. It would be no penance helping Aunt Rose around the house. She certainly had no wish to be idle all day long, and helping Aunt Rose would be something to do. It might also be one way of repaying her for a free holiday.

Kim acknowledged to herself reluctantly that Garrick Lang disturbed her much more than the thought of a little housework. That she would be seeing him again in an hour or two made her tremble. He was an attractive man, but she couldn't believe that was the only reason why she felt strangely drawn to him. She wondered if here, on Coolarie, she would get to know him better. Of course she might not get the opportunity, for all they would all be together on an isolated cattle station. He would be living in one house while she would be in another, and in spite of the fact that he and Joe were distant cousins, socially they might be poles apart.

For the time being it seemed enough that they had been together a few hours in Perth. Perth, she suspected, might be a memory she would always treasure. On the whole Garrick had been nice to her. Last night, as they had returned to the hotel, he had ordered more coffee, and whisky for himself, and they had sat and talked until well after midnight.

His amiable mood had continued over breakfast and, later, all the way to the airport. They flew from Perth to Derby, over two thousand kilometres north, by jet, and from there to Coolarie in Garrick's own plane. When Kim had first seen his private plane her eyes had widened like saucers.

'Come on, blondie,' he had teased, giving her thick plait a gentle tug, 'you must have seen a small plane before.'

'Not such a smart private one,' she confessed flushing.

'Can you fly?' he had asked, staring at her pink cheeks.

'What a question!' she had laughed. 'I can drive a car, but I've never learnt to fly. I've never had the opportunity. Does it take long?'

'A while,' he had said.

Kim hadn't pursued the matter, there seemed no point, but she had watched with great interest as he had taken off. He must use the plane to visit his other cattle stations, and she wondered wistfully if she would ever see any of them, apart from Coolarie where she was now.

As the unusual lethargy that had attacked her the previous evening crept over her, she was scarcely aware of curling against her pillows and going to sleep. While she was thinking of Garrick her eyes had closed and she drifted from reality to a dream world without realising it. She woke in alarm, drenched in sweat, to find Rose standing beside her.

'Do wake up, Kim!' she was saying fretfully. 'I expected you would be ready. Your uncle and I are waiting.'

'Oh, dear!' Kim jumped up, still feeling half dazed with tiredness. 'I'm sorry, Aunt Rose, I must have fallen asleep. I didn't mean to.'

'How tiresome!' her aunt frowned with dismay. 'Garrick does like us to be punctual.'

'I'm sorry,' Kim repeated helplessly. Hastily she

turned towards the open wardrobe to reach for a dress. 'I tell you what,' she paused as she grasped one, 'why don't you go ahead and I'll follow?'

'But what will I say?' Rose fussed.

'Just tell them the truth,' Kim replied patiently. 'I don't usually fall asleep in the middle of the day. It must be jet lag, or the change of climate or something. I'm sure I'll be all right after this.'

'But you don't know the way, dear?' Rose found something else to worry about.

'It's not dark yet.' Kim glanced out the window, trying hard to be patient. 'I promise not to get lost.'

'I'd better hear what your uncle has to say,' Rose demurred, leaving her uncertainly.

Rose left the door open and after the murmur of voices in the hall faded, Kim closed it with a sigh. She hoped Aunt Rose didn't fuss like this all the time. She seemed a bundle of nerves. Realising she was hot and sticky, she had perforce to rush to the bathroom again and take another shower. If only Aunt Rose had guessed she might have fallen asleep and looked in earlier it would have prevented Kim being late and possibly annoying Garrick and his mother.

Ten minutes later she was ready, wearing an ankle-length dress. It wasn't very glamorous, but it was thin and the soft cotton felt deliciously cool against her heated skin. Her bare feet she thrust into strapped black sandals while her hair was brushed and tied back with her favourite ribbon; there wasn't time for a more sophisticated style.

Trying to be quick, she rushed along the corridor, only to run slap into Brian's arms as he stepped from the lounge.

'Hey, be careful!' he drawled, as her flying body collided with his. 'What's the hurry?'

'I'm late!' she gasped, glancing up at him anxiously.

'I'll walk you over,' he grinned, his arms tightening. 'And don't apologise—I like little girls who throw themselves at me.'

'That won't be necessary, Brian,' a terse voice snapped behind them.

Tearing herself away from Brian, Kim shrank as she found Garrick surveying them from the doorway. She didn't want to think about what kind of construction he was putting on the scene before him, but from the look in his eyes it wasn't hard to guess. He obviously thought she was a fast worker.

'I was on my way,' she said, more curtly than she might otherwise have done, 'when I bumped into Brian.'

'Let's get going.' Garrick's unwillingness to listen to her explanation made her realise she might have phrased it better. The hand he laid on her arm hurt as through it she felt the full weight of his anger.

Brian, without another word, disappeared, leaving her to deal with Garrick alone, a task quite beyond her. She had no idea at all how to appease a man like Garrick Lang.

'You didn't have to come and fetch me,' she muttered, tripping over her feet in the fading light and only being saved from the ignominy of falling flat on her face by the continuing grip of his punishing hand.

'Are you trying to say,' he asked suavely as she regained a precarious balance, 'that you didn't appreciate me interrupting that cosy little scene in there?'

'It wasn't what you think it was!' Indignantly she felt like slapping him. 'Please Mr Lang—Garrick,' she panted, unable to keep up with him, 'you've got it all wrong. It happened exactly like I said it did.'

'Oh, and how was that?' He adjusted his long strides and the pressure he was exerting on her arm, but didn't pause. They were walking down an avenue of trees which she hadn't noticed before. Kim concluded that this must be another way to his house.

'Didn't Aunt Rose tell you?' she spluttered breathlessly. 'I fell asleep on my bed. I didn't mean to, but I must have been tired. Well, when Aunt Rose woke me she was so worried over being late, I told her to go ahead without me. I was simply trying to catch her up when I crashed into Brian in the hall.'

Garrick appeared to relax a little but after a moment snapped, 'I'd be careful of him if I were you.'

Was he trying to warn her or something? Such a bare statement aroused Kim's curiosity and a faint resentment. 'Why?' she glanced up at him warily. 'Is there any particular reason?'

His mouth tightened at her obvious inclination to question him. 'Brian likes girls, but isn't always as kind to them as he might be.'

'A lot of men aren't.'.

'So you don't object to a little rough handling?' His eyes glittered down on her as he paused.

'I didn't mean that!' she panted.

'As you're a guest on my property I won't have it.'

'Don't be silly!' She wrenched free of his hand, 'Brian's my cousin.'

'That won't deter him.'

'Well, it would me.'

He laughed in her face. 'Are you sure?'

Kim sighed, not so much angry as bewildered. 'I don't know how you can speak to me like this, Mr Lang. You scarcely know me.'

'Quite true,' he strode on, 'but I don't doubt I'll be encouraged to, unless I'm very much mistaken!'

What on earth was he talking about now? The glint in his eye made her sure he wasn't talking idly, but she didn't understand him. She decided it was best to make no comment. He didn't seem in a very good mood; perhaps he was tired. She had thought he looked tired when they had flown in from Perth.

They arrived at the house and Kim had no more time to wonder. Coming in from the semi-darkness outside, her eyes widened with surprise. Uncle Joe's house was one thing, Garrick's quite another! At a glance she took in the difference. Garrick's house was large and impressive without being ostentatious. If the hall was anything to go by, the rooms would be spacious and well furnished, everything that Joe's was not.

She was aware that the line of his mouth quirked with faint mockery. 'Do your eyes always go enormous when something startles you, Kim?'

Hastily she lowered her lids, hiding her expression. 'I—I suppose I didn't expect all this . . .'

'What did you expect when you came here?' Garrick taunted, his eyes narrowing as he stared down at her. 'Don't most young people on holiday look for romance and adventure? I imagine your head's full of wild ideas.'

Very conscious of his dark attraction, Kim was almost inclined to agree. This evening, in another well cut lounge suit, he was lean and virile, a sophisticated, all-male man. His pants and jacket didn't hide the fact that they covered a body superbly fit and well muscled. And she sensed the power in him even more, coming under the direct observation of a pair of piercing grey eyes. Her pulse quickened with an inner excitement she fought hard to disguise. She felt overwhelmed by him and wasn't sure what to do about it. Something about him made her tremble and wish crazily that she'd had more experience of men. An inexperienced little virgin would never appeal, she feared, to a man like this.

'I don't have any wild ideas in my head,' she lied rather desperately.

'I wonder?' he mused, very coolly.

Hoping feverishly that he wasn't able to read her thoughts, she strove for control of her rioting senses. 'Aren't I supposed to be meeting your mother?' she faltered, her cheeks turning pink. 'Is she with the others?'

Presenting her back to him was a mistake. She was startled to find his hands on her shoulders, whirling her back to him again. 'Kim,' he spoke with a gentle but undeniable firmness, a hint of steel, 'don't ever turn away while I'm talking to you!'

Kim hadn't bothered to bring a wrap and prayed he wouldn't notice how madly her heart was beating against the low neckline of her dress. 'Surely you'd finished?' she tried to speak lightly.

'For the moment, yes.' His grey eyes skimmed her hot face which curiously belied her indifferent tones. 'But remember you can't play the spoiled brat with me, miss! Mind your manners.'

The slight smile which came with his words might have been meant to soften them slightly, but she didn't think so. She was sure he wouldn't care whether her feelings were hurt or not?

For a few seconds he watched her throat working convulsively, the smile twisting mockingly on his sensuous mouth. 'Come,' he said at last, 'we'd better join the rest of the party before you decide to run like a scared rabbit.'

Feeling more like a trapped mouse, she allowed him to guide her gently through a heavy panelled door to the lounge.

Garrick's mother, an elderly woman with a pleasant appearance, watched their approach with sudden interest. 'Why, Rose,' she exclaimed, to Kim's aunt who was sitting beside her, 'you didn't tell me you had such an attractive niece.'

Joe looked a bit put out. 'We certainly have!' he stressed the first word of his sentence, and Kim wondered wryly if he would have been so quick to lay claim to her if she had been plain.

She stood feeling very selfconscious in her printed cotton dress, aware of Garrick's eyes deepening with amusement.

His mother enthused, 'What a lovely head of hair! It couldn't be anything else but natural.'

'My father's fair,' Kim smiled uncertainly.

'So was I,' Rose murmured ruefully. 'Once!'

To Kim's relief everyone laughed kindly and while she formally shook hands with his mother, Garrick poured her a drink before they all went in to dinner.

The dining-room was as elegant as the lounge. Kim wouldn't liked to have even tried to put a price on the furniture. Her father would adore it, the antique pieces alone might keep him enthalled for days. But in a room like this, she thought musingly, no one would dare to be other than on their best behaviour.

Meeting Garrick's speculative glance, she flushed as his eyes ran smoothly over her. An odd tension froze her limbs, holding her throat muscles taut. She felt she had been released from a pair of giant pincers, slowly squeezing the breath from her, when his mother spoke.

'Come and sit by me, Kim,' Mrs Lang commanded, 'so I can talk to you. Your aunt tells me you help your father in his shop?'

Kim smiled as she slipped into the chair beside her, at least grateful that she didn't have to sit near Garrick. She didn't appreciate the peculiar effect he had on her, but she was convinced she only needed a little time to get back on an even keel.

They had melon and a delicious thin soup. Then Garrick carved a large cut of roast beef while the housekeeper brought in dishes of vegetables and gravy. The china was gold-decorated and fragile, the cutlery silver, the glasses which held their wine good crystal. Kim was slightly bemused by it all.

During the meal Mrs Lang asked a lot of questions about England and recalled the last time she had been there herself. Rose occasionally joined in, but mostly she remained silent, while Joe and Garrick talked of station matters and compared prices in Perth with those of local markets. Whenever she glanced at the two men, which was as little as possible, Kim was conscious of a faint restraint between them.

She was just beginning to relax when Joe turned to her. Smiling jovially, he exclaimed, 'Oh, I nearly forgot! Kim can ride, Garrick, but not very well.

Would you mind checking up on her before I allow her out on her own?'

Kim glanced at her uncle with thinly veiled annoyance. Whatever had made him mention such a thing? Before tea he had happened to ask if she could ride, and she had laughed and replied, 'After a fashion.' She had added that she was in no hurry to pursue her brief acquaintance with horses as, although she liked them, she was inclined to be nervous of them. Joe should have asked her before speaking to Garrick!

'I'd rather wait,' she intervened quickly, without giving Garrick a chance to reply. 'I believe I told you, Uncle Joe, I'm in no hurry.'

Garrick ignored her as though she hadn't spoken. 'I'll see to it in the morning, Joe. There's no time like the present.'

Feeling like telling him what he could do with his suave clichés, Kim painfully bit her lip. It was difficult to make Joe or Garrick out. Joe's face expressed such genuine concern that she was almost ashamed of suspecting he was feeling extremely pleased with himself. Then she shrugged mentally. Why bother to make any further protest? If Garrick was determined to take her out, to say anything more might be a sheer waste of time.

They left early and the next morning Kim woke feeling much better. But at breakfast, after Brian had departed and while Rose was talking to someone outside, Joe startled her again by begging her not to antagonise Garrick.

'Whatever makes you think I would?' she frowned. 'At least, it's not something I would do deliberately.'

Joe glanced from his steak apologetically. 'I guess I'm imagining things,' he sighed. 'It was just something last night over dinner. You didn't always seem in sympathy with each other. I got the impression that you enjoyed opposing him.'

'But it was nothing serious,' she replied, dismayed that her wariness of Garrick had been so apparent, but knowing it would be impossible to explain that what she felt was more a kind of self-defence than antagonism. Unless that was the same thing? It was her heart she was suddenly guarding, more than anything else, but this seemed no more explainable. Rather lamely she said, 'Garrick wouldn't expect me to agree with him about everything.'

'Quite true.' Joe prodded his steak as though his appetite had deserted him. Looking up, he said wistfully, 'I wouldn't have mentioned it if it hadn't been so important.'

'Important? Why?' Kim asked gently.

'Well——' Joe hesitated. 'Oh, I can't really bother you with my troubles on your first morning, Kim. I—we hardly know each other, and you're so young.'

'Not that young, Uncle Joe,' she exclaimed rather sharply. And because he seemed both tired and anxious, she found herself deviating a little from what was strictly the truth. 'We may not know each other very well, but surely blood is thicker than water?'

'Of course,' his smile was quite movingly wistful, 'I might have known you'd be as understanding. All the same,' he sighed, 'it isn't something I would have concerned you about if it hadn't been for your aunt. You see, Kim, I'm not far off retirement and I'm hoping that if I keep on the right side of Garrick he might offer me a little extra pension, perhaps a few shares in the company or something.'

'I'd have thought you'd have had something like that already,' Kim remarked impulsively.

Joe shrugged wryly. 'I did have once,' he confessed with obvious reluctance, 'but I had to sell them when your aunt was very ill a few years ago. She needed special treatment.'

To Kim this didn't seem fair. Shouldn't Garrick have paid for that? It also seemed to imply that he underpaid his manager, if Joe had to rely on special reserves for anything extra. However, she was wise enough to realise that Joe might not have told her the whole story, and it might be prudent to be cautious.

'What will you do when you do retire?' she asked tactfully.

'I'm not sure,' Joe hedged unhappily, watching her closely as he referred again to his depleted finances. 'It will probably depend on what I can afford. Rose often talks of a house on the coast, but we could be getting too ambitious.'

Though this didn't seem over-ambitious to Kim, she doubted if her attitude would in any way influence any decision Garrick might make regarding Joe's retirement. It was only to set Joe's mind at rest that she promised to do nothing, if she could help it, to upset Garrick. It wouldn't be too impossible a task to be pleasant when he was around, she thought wryly. Already she liked him so much she found it difficult to stop thinking about him. If she wasn't careful, being nice to him might become her sole ambition in life.

Nodding with relief and restored good humour, Joe drank his second cup of coffee and left for the office. Kim finished hers and began helping Rose with the housework. There wasn't a lot to do and they might have got through it quite quickly if Rose hadn't complained frequently of a headache and each time begged Kim to make her a cup of tea. After she had finished preparing lunch—following Rose's instructions—her aunt asked if she would mind taking a message to Joe. She would have gone herself, Rose said apologetically, but she still didn't feel well, and if Kim could amuse herself for an hour or two she would go and lie down.

Knowing her aunt might be able to relax better if she was out of the house, Kim set off willingly. Finding Joe wasn't difficult as she went in the general direction of the spread of buildings, and there was a large, very noticeable sign over the office door. But frequently, before she reached it, Kim paused to gaze around. The land about the station seemed a mixture of reds, browns and greens, mostly the former. She decided the blazing splashes of colour must be the profusion of spring flowers Garrick had spoken of. Although she knew she was in a great pastoral area between the Kimberleys and the Fitzroy River, she was amazed by the breadth and apparent endlessness of it. In England the horizon never seemed that far away; here she was sure it was limitless miles. The sun blazed down, but her whole being seemed to stretch out to welcome it, like a cat. The air might be hot, but it was clean and sweet, wonderful to a girl too used to being cooped up inside all day. Not that she didn't love the shop, Kim appeased her guilty conscience hastily, but freedom such as a landscape like this presented was enchanting!

The office door was open. Someone moved inside as she stood for yet another moment drinking in all the marvellous, breathtaking space. 'I'd better be careful,' she called laughingly to Joe. 'If I see too much of this I shan't want to go home.'

'No doubt you will, when the time comes?' a deep voice replied, as she stepped into the office.

'Garrick!' She was struck by surprise. He was sitting on the edge of the desk, idly watching her. Her eyes, fluttering uncertainly to avoid his, assessed the casual attire he was wearing. She hadn't seen him dressed like this before. His checked shirt was open several buttons from the neck, exposing dark, curling body hair, while tight cotton jeans moulded the powerful curve of his thighs, making no secret of the strength of his long, muscled legs. Feeling a quivering stir of something nameless creeping over her, Kim gulped and looked quickly at Joe.

'Aunt Rose wondered if you would get in touch with Bennets, in town, and ask if her new chair covers are ready yet.'

'She's been bothered about those ever since she knew you were coming,' Joe sighed, 'but I'll see to it.' He flicked through a sheaf of papers, as if to indicate he was busy.

Sliding off the desk, Garrick came over to Kim, his

eyes still doing their own inventory. 'Good morning,' he smiled mockingly. 'I too am capable of appreciating what I can see, and you're looking particularly charming. All you need is a hat, which we can get from the stores, then I'll take you riding.'

'Oh, please, there's no need.' His rather deliberate speech made her uneasy, as did the thoughtful glint in his eye. Aware that the rustle of Joe's paper had become a disapproving silence, she was reminded of her promise to him, but she was sure there was nothing objectionable in what she had just said.

'There's every need,' Garrick clipped adamantly. 'As Joe was saying last night, it's important that I see exactly what you're capable of.'

'Aren't you too busy?' Ignoring Joe's strident cough, which was no doubt a further attempt to remind her of her obligations, she went on protesting. 'I don't want to be a nuisance.'

'Now when is a pretty girl ever that?' Garrick quipped lazily, taking her arm with a brief nod to Joe and guiding her firmly from the office.

CHAPTER THREE

OUTSIDE the office, still filled with a nameless apprehension, Kim pulled against the drag of Garrick's hand on her arm. Escape routes might be few, and she settled for the first one she could think of. 'Shouldn't I fetch a jacket?'

Garrick laughed, as if guessing what she was up to. 'You aren't at home now, Kim, in a climate blessed—you often think cursed—by constant showers. As we aren't in the Wet yet, you won't need a jacket.'

When his eyes went impassively over her, despite the blankness of his expression, she felt hot enough to do without even the tee-shirt she was wearing. For what seemed the hundredth time she wondered how he could so easily disturb her. In the shop many men had subjected her to a much closer scrutiny and her pulse had never beat even a little faster. In the stores, as Garrick sardonically clamped a hat on her pale head, she tried not to notice the feelings his fingers aroused as he adjusted the strap under her small, rounded chin.

To her surprise the horses were saddled and waiting.

'I was just about to call for you at the house,' said Garrick. Placing his hands on her wais, he startled her by lifting her bodily on to the back of a smart little mare. She felt his strong arms tense, but that was all; she might have been weightless. The chestnut stirred, sidestepping a little, but at a word from Garrick, was still again.

Kim couldn't keep from asking smartly, 'Shouldn't you have waited to see if I was capable of mounting myself?'

'You did say you had some experience,' he reminded

her mildly, 'and getting on is usually the first thing one learns. I was just trying to save time.'

Colouring faintly, she shrugged. With Garrick she never seemed able to win! 'Perhaps I didn't believe you would take my word for it,' she murmured.

'Now why should you think that, I wonder?' he retorted softly.

Kim didn't answer, but watched as he mounted his own horse, a splendid stallion, several hands higher than the mare she was on. Her breath caught as she saw how formidable the horse and man looked together. A powerful, unbeatable combination! Nervously she moistened her lips, averting her eyes from Garrick's compelling figure.

Later, as he allowed her to canter over open country, she dared to ask what he thought of her.

He turned his head and smiled teasingly. 'I presume you're referring to your riding?'

She released an exasperated sigh. 'Of course.'

His smile deepened. 'I just wanted to make sure I wasn't getting involved in a very personal question. There's nothing wrong with the way you're handling your horse. Initially, I think, you had a good teacher. All you require is a lot more practice and confidence.'

'I realise that,' she nodded. 'A girl friend taught me, and she's very good. Her father has a property near the town where I live, but I don't get the chance of going there very often, and I don't have a horse of my own.'

'Joe says you work long hours in your father's business?'

Garrick rode slightly behind her, she could feel his eyes on her constantly as if, for all his general approval, he wasn't yet ready to leave her in unsupervised possession of one of his valuable animals. She wondered how Joe knew about the kind of hours she worked, and decided her mother must have mentioned it in a letter, for she certainly hadn't said anything herself.

'My parents go to a lot of auction sales,' she replied somewhat stiffly. 'Sometimes they're gone all day.'

'You're very young to be left in charge.'

'Plenty people my age are running their own business,' she pointed out. 'And if we're particularly busy we can always find someone to come in.'

'You have a lot of unemployed,' he observed soberly.

'Too many,' she agreed. 'I have friends who've never had a job and all they want to do is work. It's terrible for them—and some people have the nerve to say they don't look hard enough!'

'There are those who never understand,' he said gravely.

'Nor do they seem to want to!' she retorted bitterly.

Garrick said little more until they reached the shelter of a group of trees. There weren't many trees, she noticed. Although the countryside in the distance was ruggedly mountainous, mostly the ground they had travelled over was brown and dry and very open. Following Garrick's directions it proved easy riding but he did warn her about some of the things to look out for if she was ever out alone. He called them natural hazards, the desert grass, the spinifex, which could grow four feet high and was full of spikes which could stick in the flesh, making it itch and burn. And the mulga, dense thickets of impenetrable bush which might rip a horse and rider to pieces if they tried to go directly through it.

'Desert country can be a friend or foe,' he told her, 'depending on how well you know it and how you treat it. It pays to treat it with respect.'

Stopping under some ghost gums, they dismounted, and after tethering the horses, Garrick took her arm and showed her a boab, or bottle tree. Its huge, squat trunk was hollow inside, and he told her they had been known to be used as temporary jails in the early days.

'How awful!' Kim exclaimed, glancing at him indignantly. 'I wish you hadn't shown it to me.'

'I forgot about your warm heart,' he glanced at her with a mocking smile in his grey eyes as they returned to the horses. 'How is it you aren't married? Or does marriage seem like a prison to you as well?'

When she merely shook her head, he refused to be satisfied with such a negative response. He rephrased his question lightly. 'Haven't you met anyone you would like to marry yet, Kim?'

'No!' As her heartbeats faltered and then began to race, she assured herself desperately it was the truth. She might be developing some kind of infatuation for Garrick Lang, but like measles and chickenpox it would soon clear up. If she was clever he needn't even guess.

Hating the slow smile spreading across his face, she knew an urgent desire to retaliate. 'No,' she repeated, making sure he understood. 'Have you?'

His eyes narrowed, as if he considered she was taking liberties, then he relaxed. 'I'll only admit that you have as much right to ask.'

Disliking his deviousness, she felt resentful. 'At least I gave you an answer.'

'So you did,' he drawled with teasing amusement, 'and now you believe I owe you one?'

'Well, don't you?'

Leaning one arm lazily along the branch of a tree, he looked down on her. 'I have no respect for idle curiosity. A lot of women want to know why I've never married, but some of them have been in love with me.'

'How nice—but how can you be sure?' she mocked lightly.

'They told me.'

Kim's eyes widened. 'Well, if they did, you shouldn't be callous enough to sound amused. Didn't you love any of them back?'

He replied mockingly, 'Occasionally I've had the urge to make love to them, but never anything more than that. I've certainly never had any desire to present anyone with a wedding ring.'

A bird, more colourful than anything she had seen before, fluttered in the branches of the tree, but Kim scarcely noticed it. Her vision was too filled with the big man beside her. His frank confession that he enjoyed making love to women shocked her slightly, but it also excited. She forced herself to stick to more practical issues.

Staring down on the ground, she queried, 'Doesn't a man like you need a wife to help him socially?'

His eyes glinted. 'You wouldn't be trying to persuade me?'

'No, of course not!' She jumped as though she had been stung, her cheeks scarlet. 'We've only just met!'

'So we have,' his brows rose in mock surprise, 'and here we are, conversing like old friends. Which must bear out the old saying that it's easier to talk to strangers.' When Kim flinched visibly, he looked faintly ashamed of himself. 'I'm sorry, Kim, but the truth is I'm never in the same place very long. A month here, a month there, cattle sales and shows, business meetings in most of the capital cities. I'm also a breeder and export stud animals, which can mean shooting off to practically any corner of the earth at a moment's notice. Would it be fair to ask any woman to share that?'

'Couldn't she go with you?'

'Fine,' he agreed curtly, 'until the children begin to arrive.'

'You sound as if your pocket might stretch to a nanny,' she replied dryly.

He considered her, his eyes taunting. 'Half a dozen, if that would solve the problem, but I doubt it. Women, being the maternal creatures they are, rarely want to be parted from their offspring for more than a day or two.'

'Don't have any, then,' she advised rashly.

Leisurely his gaze roamed over her. 'Would you agree to a proposition like that?'

Fearing she might not, she swallowed, her throat

suddenly dry as her breathing quickened unconsciously. Hastily she said, 'Perhaps you should stick to your affairs.'

'I've been happy to, until now,' his eyes glinted, 'though don't imagine I have them one after another, or that they last any length of time. Until now I haven't been interested in anything more permanent.'

Startled, Kim felt her cheeks grow hot. Could he possibly be hinting at herself? Then as swiftly came the answer. No, of course not! 'You mean you have a girl-friend at the moment?'

'I'm not sure,' he laughed a little harshly.

So he wasn't giving anything away. She avoided his eyes carefully, well aware of the dangers of getting too deeply involved. If Garrick really set his mind to it, he might be able to seduce her, but unless she encouraged him she sensed she would be quite safe. Especially as he had partly confessed to being interested in another woman.

With the events of the morning beginning to catch up on her, she kept her eyes fixed on the red earth at their feet, moving in a kind of weary daze. The silence between them lengthened, then Garrick took her hand in the hot sunshine. Turning her towards him, he gently removed her riding hat. Letting it slide to the ground, he put his arms around her, and drawing her closer, he firmly tilted up her chin.

Kim was aware of his every deliberate movement, but despite her former foreboding she found she had no desire to fight him. This might all be happening too soon, but she had always known that if ever she met a man she really liked she would find it difficult to pretend to be indifferent. This was why, when Garrick took her in his arms, she smiled very faintly. It wasn't a flirtatious smile—she just wanted him to know she wasn't frightened.

His quizzical glance met hers with a hint of amusement. 'Aren't you going to struggle or hit me, or something?'

'If I did,' she managed, 'it might only encourage you!'

'You could always try that well-worn line about not being that kind of girl.'

Kim was suddenly nervous, as something indefinable in his expression warned her she might be wise to follow up one of his suggestions. It took a lot of will-power to remain quietly where she was. 'I don't think I'm the kind of girl you had in mind when you said that!' she retorted.

His brows rose mockingly. 'At least you're very self-possessed! I'm not sure whether to be flattered or not. If I'd made any impression, shouldn't you be trembling in my arms?'

'So far you've done nothing to make me.' While forcing herself to copy his light tones, she hoped he didn't notice her racing pulse. She had no great faith in the self-possession he spoke of, so swiftly was he turning her to a mass of quivering jelly.

'So the fault is mine? Very remiss of me,' he smiled lazily, pulling her closer as he slowly lowered his mouth to touch her soft lips.

Kim's reaction was not as she had planned, as she was unable to control her natural one. She had told the truth when she had hinted that she didn't go in for casual kissing, but in the split second before Garrick's mouth descended she realised she had been foolish to be so flippant about it. He hadn't taken her seriously, he probably imagined she expected something more satisfying than a brief embrace. But she knew instinctively that he was no easily handled young boy of her own age. He was all man and might easily demand more than a few light kisses.

The encircling band of his arms tightened sharply until she felt crushed. Something brutal in their sudden pressure sent burning sensations shooting right through her and her breath stopped as she waited for her submissive lips to receive the same kind of treatment. She spread her trapped fingers across his chest

in mute protest, trying to push him away, while a kind
of wild, delirious joy rushed through her. Then she
trembled as his mouth parted hers ruthlessly, igniting
flames of excitement where before her emotions had
merely smouldered.

For a brief moment he devoured her lips passionately
while his hands slid to her waist and hips, exploring
the slender contours of her body with sensual
thoroughness. Desire flared, then she was put from
him so swiftly she felt bereft. The blood in her veins
had begun singing, in heady anticipation of expected
pleasure. She had gone boneless and pliant, her arms
struggling to creep round his neck. Now she knew a
deep sense of rejection. She was like someone deprived
of a promised treat, and her eyes betrayed her fleeting
bewilderment even as her lips formed an unconscious,
'Why?'

When something flickered in his eyes and his hands
lifted as though to reach for her again, she was swept
by a heady sense of power—to think he could resist
her no more than she could resist him! She nearly
moaned aloud as his hands dropped back to his sides
and he simply shook his head, his face set in stern,
unapproachable lines.

'You won't have to ask that in a week or two, my
child, if you continue as you are doing.' Very slightly
his fingers tipped her face, enabling him to see her
flushed cheeks and puzzled eyes. 'If it's a holiday affair
you're after, I'm not saying I wouldn't be willing to
oblige, but I must give you time to be sure you know
what it is you do want, and to know exactly what you
would be taking on.'

He sounded so flatly reasonable, Kim didn't understand the hidden threat. And it was there, she was sure.
Somehow she suspected he had deliberately brought
her here, this morning, for some reason not altogether
connected with the words he had just uttered.
Suddenly she was convinced he had meant to frighten
her, and in some way his intentions had rebounded on

himself. It was becoming increasingly clear that he knew or suspected something of which she had no knowledge. Was it to do with Brian? she wondered. Did Garrick believe she might be in danger of falling for her cousin and imagine a few kisses from him might prevent it? It could be, yet nothing seemed that simple. Not even the memory of Garrick's anger when he thought he had caught her in Brian's arms seemed enough to wholly support a theory like that.

They rode back to the homestead in silence, Kim still feeling slightly dazed, not totally in touch with reality. But despite her prevailing fears she wasn't completely unhappy. She supposed everything would fall in place eventually. For the moment Garrick's presence, the sun and the thought of being with him a while longer seemed enough. She might have to worry about the future in six months' time, but, right now, six months seemed a million years away.

The only uneasiness to mar the homeward journey was caused by the fleeting glimpse she occasionally caught of Garrick's face. He continued to ride slightly behind her, and once or twice, on turning her head, she thought he looked quite savage.

At the homestead he asked if she would care to join him for lunch as it was after two and Rose and Joe would have finished theirs by this time. Kim thanked him, but refused. He had been obliged to invite her to dinner the night before. She didn't want him to feel she was becoming a nuisance.

He nodded, as if he didn't mind one way or another, but she hadn't gone more than a few yards before he called her back.

'You're making me quite absent-minded,' a half smile relaxed the grim lines of his mouth. 'My mother asked me to ask you if you'd like to have tea with her later on. About four will do.'

Kim hesitated, her voice husky, 'Your mother doesn't have to be kind to me.'

'No,' his eyes contained a faint amusement, 'she

doesn't, but from what I gather the boot could be on the other foot. She intends you should be kind to her. She wants to go into town tomorrow, and hopes you might be willing to drive her there.'

'Why, I'd love to,' Kim felt a glow of pleasure, 'but I—well, if she has a regular driver, wouldn't I be doing someone out of a job?'

'She usually drives herself,' Garrick replied, 'but she hurt her arm a few weeks ago and it still aches if she uses it for any length of time. It's still painful and stiff, and I know driving aggravates the condition.'

'In that case I'd love to oblige,' Kim assured him gravely, 'but she doesn't have to invite me to tea.'

He glanced quickly at the watch strapped to his hair-sprinkled wrist. 'I haven't time to argue, Kim, just be there.'

'All right,' she agreed, staring after him longer than she realised, as with a brief nod of his dark head he finally left her.

Aunt Rose didn't appear at all upset that Kim was late for lunch. 'There's plenty of meat and salad,' she laughed. 'Midday, in this climate, I can never face anything hot. The only thing I enjoy hot is a cup of coffee.'

Kim helped herself, surprised to discover how hungry she was. There was ham, pink and tender, and the salad was crisp and delicious. While she ate she told her aunt that she had enjoyed her outing with Garrick very much. 'I'll probably be too stiff to move in the morning, though,' she said ruefully.

'Oh, dear, I hope not!' Rose exclaimed in mock dismay. 'The shop has my new covers ready to pick up and I was wondering if you could drive me to town tomorrow to collect them.'

'Yes, of course,' Kim smiled at her aunt, whom she was pleased to see looking so much better. Then suddenly she remembered Mrs Lang. 'Oh, I almost forgot,' she exclaimed, 'I believe Garrick's mother would like me to take her in, too.'

'That won't matter,' Rose said happily. 'She won't mind me. I often go along just to keep her company. I enjoy a trip out occasionally, especially as your Uncle Joe rarely has time to take me anywhere.'

While Kim cleared away her luncheon dishes Rose told her about the various towns in the area and the one nearest to them. Kim refused coffee in favour of orange squash, then after drinking it she decided to go and have a shower before going to see Mrs Lang. It was very hot, but she didn't find it tiring. The ride this morning with Garrick had been invigorating, and although he hadn't said anything about taking her out again, she hoped he would. Wryly she confessed to herself that she would much rather go riding with him than visiting any number of towns.

Whenever she thought of him her heart began increasing its beat, and she was aware that she must have looked glowing when she returned to lunch. It slightly puzzled her that Aunt Rose hadn't warned her about him. Garrick being older and more experienced, it wouldn't have seemed unreasonable if Rose had been concerned for fear her niece should fall for him and perhaps go home with a broken heart. Rose must have decided that Garrick was too far beyond Kim's reach for there to be any possibility of that happening, so it wasn't worth mentioning. Still, Kim wondered.

In broad daylight, Garrick's house impressed Kim even more than it had done the evening before. The gardens were well kept and green from constant watering. Trees lined the paths while some had been grown in groups to break up flat areas. There were plenty of flowers and near the end of the garden she saw a tennis court alongside a pavilion, behind which she suspected there might be a swimming-pool.

Avoiding the front entrance, Kim slipped around to the rear door, reluctant that anyone should think she thought of herself as an honoured guest. The housekeeper welcomed her with a friendly smile and said no, Kim wasn't late, she was just in time, she was just taking tea through. And Mrs Lang was expecting her.

Mrs Lang was in the lounge. 'Come in, Kim,' she smiled, looking up from a letter she was busy reading. 'How nice of you to take pity on an old lady!'

Kim heard the housekeeper sniff and felt amused. She didn't believe Mrs Lang would ever seem an old lady, not even when she was one. She had such an active mind and the same vital, alive expression which she had obviously passed on to her son. Not much would escape either of them, Kim was sure.

The housekeeper refused to join them for tea. 'I've a new recipe I want to study over mine, and I'll do that better in the kitchen.'

'Abby's a dear,' Mrs Lang said when she went. 'I don't know what I should do without her.'

'It must be rather lonely for you here when Garrick's away,' Kim observed politely.

Mrs Lang waved her to a chair. 'Yes and no,' she replied briskly. 'I have plenty of friends and travel myself, occasionally. Garrick and I don't believe in being too dependent on one another. I must confess, though, that I look forward to the day he takes a wife. I'd love to see this house filled with my grand-children.'

Kim lowered her lashes to stop her surprise showing. Didn't Mrs Lang know her son's views on that subject? 'There's certainly enough room,' she replied evasively. Then, feeling guiltily ashamed of herself for taking advantage of a mother's natural eagerness to talk about her family, she asked, 'Hasn't Garrick anyone in mind?'

'Not that I know of,' Mrs Lang sighed. 'There are plenty of girls who would marry him tomorrow, but none whom he seems keen to settle down with. I'll just have to wait and see.'

Kim picked up her teacup, determined to be circumspect. Mrs Lang might be willing to answer the odd question about her son, but she doubted if she would discuss him at any length.

She murmured that the tea was delicious, and Mrs Lang nodded and told her to help herself to cake. She began talking about her shoulder, and Kim admired her for making light of it.

'I'm having treatment,' Mrs Lang explained, 'but it will take time. If you could drive me to town in the morning, it would be a great help.'

Kim said she would be pleased to take her anywhere, any time. She mentioned Aunt Rose.

'Of course she can come,' Mrs Lang smiled. 'I hope she told you she doesn't need to ask.'

'Yes.' Abby's chocolate cake melted in Kim's mouth, and she wondered if she dared ask for another slice. 'It's a pity Aunt Rose never learnt to drive, because I expect my uncle and Brian are usually too busy to take her anywhere.'

A slightly guarded expression replaced the smile on Mrs Lang's face. 'Well, I do try and make sure she's never stuck for want of transport. Your uncle rarely leaves Coolarie unless it's to do something of his own, and your cousin is often gone for weeks at a time.'

Kim glanced at her quickly. Mrs Lang's voice was impersonal, but surely there was a hint of censure?

'Does Brian visit your other stations?' She added hastily, as Mrs Lang looked at her curiously, 'Garrick told me about them.'

'No, he doesn't,' Mrs Lang replied sharply, as if the subject was distasteful to her. 'It wouldn't be so bad if he did. No one knows where he gets to and he often disappears when he's most needed. His father doesn't approve, naturally, but he isn't apparently able to do anything about it. One of these days I sometimes think he won't come home again. So far he has.'

If Kim had already sensed all was not well with her aunt's family, she had decided it was none of her business. Even the nicest of families had their problems. They had them at home. Mrs Lang hinted at something more than the usual domestic squabble which cleared the air and could be easily forgotten, but Kim felt reluctant to talk about it. If it was anything very serious, surely Aunt Rose would eventually tell her about it herself.

Kim was saved from having to answer by Garrick. When he walked in his mother looked surprised. 'I didn't expect to see you!' she exclaimed.

Garrick smiled and sank lazily on a sofa beside them. 'I got back sooner than I expected.' He turned his head to study Kim in her blue cotton sundress, a dress she mightn't have worn if she had known he was to be here. The narrow straps exposed a great deal of bare skin which his eyes were exploring with a cool but close interest; she felt them slide down the V between her breasts as though he were physically touching her. Did he always show such mocking interest in girls he had only known a day or two?

There was something calculating in his glance too, she noted, but her indignation quickly faded as his eyes returned to her face and he smiled at her. Who could resist him when he turned on the charm? She just wanted to drown in his cloud-grey pupils when he stared into her blue eyes.

He had to break the contact when he accepted a cup of tea from his mother, but Kim soon had his attention again. 'I found a message from your uncle in the office, Kim. He's taken Rose to town for her covers and something to eat. They won't be home until later.'

'Oh!' Bewilderment jerked Kim from the trance she was in, this and Mrs Lang's gasp of astonishment. 'I'd better go home,' she blurted in confusion. 'If Aunt Rose is away there'll be no one to cook Brian's dinner.'

'Message from him, too,' Garrick relayed coolly, never taking his eyes from her face. 'He's gone to Port Hedland, until tomorrow.'

'I see,' she whispered, not seeing at all.

'So do I, I think,' she thought she heard Garrick mutter under his breath, but when she looked at him with anxious enquiry, he merely looked back at her with a strange light in his eyes.

'You'd better have dinner with us again, Kim. No sense in spending the evening alone in an empty house.'

Mrs Lang said absently but quite kindly, 'Yes, do, dear.'

Feeling trapped, Kim was about to murmur a word of thanks when a voice called from the hall, 'Anyone at home?'

Through the open door came a tall, well made brunette, beautifully made-up and dressed. Glancing down at her simple cotton dress, Kim sighed.

'Hello, Aunt Jessica, how cosy!' The brunette's glance skipped from the tea tray to Garrick. 'Hello, darling. Since when did you become addicted to afternoon tea?'

'I'm very fond of it, when I get the chance,' he grinned, rising to his feet as the girl waltzed over to him. This was the only way Kim could describe such affected, sinuous movements. Reaching up, the stranger kissed Garrick full on the mouth, leaving a generous deposit of bright red lipstick. 'I heard you were home, darling, so I just had to drop by.'

'Nice of you, Irene.' Disentangling himself, Garrick took a handkerchief from his pocket to scrub the red gloss from his mouth, a faint gleam of amusement in his eyes.

'It's nice to see you,' Mrs Lang smiled at Irene warmly. 'Come and sit down and tell us what you've been doing.'

As Irene obliged, Kim noticed Mrs Lang made no attempt to pour her a cup of tea. She didn't wonder any longer, however, when Garrick placed a large whisky and soda in the girl's hands. This told Kim that the dazzling brunette was very sophisticated and that both Garrick and his mother must be very familiar with her habits.

Mrs Lang quickly introduced Kim. 'Irene dear, this is Miss Grantley, Rose's niece from England. Kim, Mrs Ross.'

Irene's cool smile froze, her brown eyes flickering over Kim with a distaste she didn't try to hide. 'Really?' Averting her eyes indifferently, she spoke to Mrs Lang. 'How interesting. Is she staying long?'

The hand Kim tentatively held out fell back to her side. For some reason Mrs Ross had no desire to look at her, let alone touch her. She wondered where the husband was. Or perhaps Mrs Ross was divorced, or even a widow. When Garrick intervened idly to say that Kim might be staying as long as six months, Irene Ross went quite pale.

Kim watched, wide-eyed, as he sat down beside her and whispered something, smilingly, in her ear. Whatever it was, Kim couldn't help noticing it cheered Irene up, and she began looking pleased with herself again. Happily she continued sipping her drink while her free hand began tracing, as if unconsciously, the hard-packed muscles of Garrick's thigh. Kim followed the movements of those long brown fingers and tried not to feel sick.

Presently, as the talk became general, Irene said, 'I thought if you did happen to be around, Garrick, and you are, we might have had a game of tennis before dinner.'

Deciding this let her out, Kim jumped to her feet. 'I think I'd better go home, after all.'

Garrick looked at her gravely. 'Do you play tennis, Kim?'

She smiled ruefully. 'Yes, but I haven't played much since leaving school.'

Irene frowned, as if the implication of Garrick's query didn't please her, then she smiled craftily as she caught his hand. 'Why not invite her to join us darling? We must be kind to our overseas visitors, mustn't we? And especially when they're related to Joe!'

'I was just about to.' With a sharp glance at Irene, he freed his hand and went to Kim. Towering over her, he gave instructions which she couldn't find the courage to disobey. 'Run home and change into a pair of shorts,' he said, 'then come back and join us in the garden. The tennis courts are very easy to find.'

Kim had brought a pair of shorts from England. They were the ones she had worn for games at school. In the years since, her legs must have grown longer and slimmer, for now the shorts seemed incredibly short and wide. Having no time to do anything about them, she belted them around her narrow waist as best she could before trailing reluctantly back to the big house. Was Garrick in love with Mrs Ross? Kim prayed not. She knew, although she scarcely dared put it in words, not even in her mind, that she wanted him to be in love with no one but herself. She wanted this so much it was beginning to hurt!

Close up the tennis courts were just as impressive as they had seemed from a distance. Irene and Garrick were waiting for her. As she approached they must have heard her footsteps, for they both turned, Irene to examine Kim's slender young figure insolently.

'If you played more tennis and swam occasionally, you might develop a few more inches. You look as if a breath of wind might blow you away!'

'Except in places,' Garrick teased.

Kim turned her head, on its long willowy neck, so they mightn't see her mounting colour. 'I'm afraid in England we don't get all this lovely hot weather,' she replied stiffly.

'That's one way of describing it,' Irene drawled dryly. Turning to Garrick, she suggested, 'How about finding Brian and making up a set of doubles?'

'Brian has gone to Port Hedland,' Garrick said abruptly.

'He has?' Irene made Kim curious by betraying a quick anger which she immediately disguised. Only a hint of it remained in her voice as she cried sharply, 'I don't know why you put up with him, Garrick darling!'

'Perhaps because he's a sort of cousin, like you,' Garrick replied sardonically.

So Irene was related, if not closely. Kim felt she might have guessed from Irene's behaviour. It depressed Kim to see the way the other girl hung on Garrick's arm, almost as if she couldn't stand without his support.

Kim had learnt that Irene was a widow. On her way to find her shorts, she had gone through the kitchen again. When she had explained briefly what she was going to do, Abby had asked rather shortly if she knew if Irene was leaving or staying for dinner. When she had answered uncomfortably that she believed Mrs Ross might be staying, Abby had merely sighed and said that as Irene was a widow she supposed she had nothing to go home for.

If Irene was a widow now, Kim pondered, staring abstractedly towards the hazy horizon, did she hope to make Garrick her second husband? It certainly looked that way!

CHAPTER FOUR

BECOMING vaguely aware of the other two arguing idly, Kim jerked her attention back to what they were busy discussing. It was decided that Irene and Kim should play first and that Garrick should take on the winner.

Of course Kim lost hopelessly. She was no match for Irene's deadly service and driving backhanders. She was soon scuttling wildly around the court, with no very clear idea in her head as to what she was doing, and the few balls she did manage to return went completely outside the white markings. Irene played viciously, not bothering to hide her contempt when Kim's hair became loosened from its ponytail, making her game worse as it swung across her hot face, almost blinding her.

Knowing that Australians took their tennis very seriously helped Kim to believe there was nothing personal in the furious way Irene routed her. It must be her own fault for agreeing to play in the first place. She supposed Garrick's eyes followed her constantly because she was making such a fool of herself and he was delighting in Irene's victory.

When his turn came she tried not to enjoy seeing him beat Irene to a frazzle. She also tried not to believe he had played a deliberately punishing game in order to avenge Rose's young niece. When Irene admitted defeat, having scored no points whatsoever, Kim felt quite sorry for the older girl; she looked both bewildered and faintly annoyed.

'Your game has certainly improved since I played with you last, Garrick darling,' she said silkily.

'Maybe I never tried before,' he replied a shade curtly, placing a hand under Kim's elbow to lift her to her feet. 'Come on,' he smiled briefly, 'let's all have a swim and cool off before dinner.'

In the pool, in a two-piece costume borrowed from the changing rooms, Kim fared little better than she had done on the tennis court. Irene swam superbly, but this time Kim didn't even try to compete. After slowly circling the pool she contented herself with staying at the shallow end, splashing gently in the water. Irene swam as though she was trying to prove something, and ruefully Kim suspected it might be her own inadequacy. Like her tennis, she had had little chance to improve it since leaving school.

Irene, as long as Kim kept out of her way, chose to ignore her, but Garrick returned to her side frequently, and Kim wasn't sure if that was a good thing. When he was close, his keen gaze trained on her, she felt absurdly conscious of the two tiny pieces of gauzy cotton she was wearing. As fast as the water cooled her heated skin, his mocking glance warmed it again. And when he reared up beside her she was terribly conscious of his powerful, trim physique, his broad shoulders, narrow hips and long thrusting legs. He made her feel breathless when she was barely moving and she was terrified he might see just how fast her heart was beating.

In his brief trunks, as black as his black hair, she imagined he found it easy to make a girl tremble. And tremble Kim certainly did when once he accidently touched her. What was the matter with her? she asked herself crossly, ignoring the answer. Why didn't she laugh and say something smart instead of blinking at him with huge, entreating eyes? What was she pleading for, anyway? Mercy? Where Garrick Lang was concerned that might be a futile hope. He had a measure of cruelty in his personality, she was sure, even if it was hidden most of the time behind lazy, heavy-lidded eyes. While she was willing to be obedient and submissive, he might treat her gently, but step one inch out of line and she might feel the full length of his mental whip, if not a more visible one.

'Are you all right?' His arm curved around her waist, and she hadn't realised she had gone quite pale until he spoke.

'Yes,' she nodded quickly, thinking she must be taking leave of her senses. Angrily she dived away from him, unfortunately before remembering to close her mouth, and succeeded in swallowing about a gallon of water and was forced to climb choking out the other side.

'Please tell your mother I'll make something for myself at Aunt Rose's house,' she gasped, her eyes widening in alarm as he came up behind her again. Fascinated, her glance slid down his dripping body and her breath stopped.

'Seen enough?' he drawled, 'or not?'

Colour rushed to her face, brought there as much by her own stupidity as his taunting tones. 'Did—did you hear what I said?' she stammered, overwhelmed by embarrassment.

'No, I didn't,' he snapped, 'I'm deaf! Just get back here as soon as you like, once you're dressed again. Or I'll come and drag you out, if necessary.'

The humiliating implications of that, and the steel-soft voice with which the ultimatum was delivered, proved too much for Kim. As his eyes sought her face and the sensual tension between them leapt like a live thing, she smothered a strangled cry and fled.

The evening that followed was for Kim a strange mixture of stress and despair, but it did have its moments of near happiness. The despair came from listening to Irene and being brought to realise that Irene had known Garrick all her life, so knew far more about him than ever she was likely to. The happiness Kim derived came mostly from Garrick's frequent glances in her direction, the occasional warmth of his gaze, his deliberate determination to include her in the conversation when Irene would have shut her out.

This irritated Irene so much that she obviously

decided to punish Garrick by leaving early. As he saw her politely to her car, Kim muttered a hurried excuse to Mrs Lang and left too.

Abby wasn't around as she slipped through the back of the house, but her efforts were wasted, as Garrick caught up with her before she had got very far.

'What's the hurry?' he asked, one brow raised in enquiring mockery.

'It's been a long day,' she tried to ignore his demanding arrogance, 'and I'm sure if Uncle Joe and Aunt Rose aren't home yet they soon will be.'

He took her arm companionably. 'I'll come with you and see.'

At his touch a flicker of raw emotion sliced through her and she stiffened. 'There's no need.'

He slanted her a wry glance through the star-strewn darkness. 'Can't you forget those three words?'

Kim sighed, strangely content, now the first impact had subsided, to have his hand cupping her elbow and his faintly smiling face towering above her. 'I thought you'd be saying goodnight to Mrs Ross.'

'So I did,' he drawled, his fingers tightening a punishing fraction, 'which only involved seeing her to her car.'

As this didn't seem to imply that they had lingered in the shadow of it, Kim felt wonderfully warm again. A happy smile lit her face as she lifted it towards the sky. 'Your stars are really amazing—much brighter than they are at home. It doesn't seem fair,' she added humorously.

'You must stop comparing everything here with what you have at home,' he replied idly, appearing more interested in her face than the stars above it. 'It's different, that's all. Think of your green and pleasant land. Australia, especially in areas like this, can be a harsh, arid place to live in. We have days when the temperature rarely drops below a hundred and a man begins to wonder if it could ever be fair to ask a woman to share it with him.'

'I like the heat,' said Kim without thinking.

'That wouldn't be a kind of roundabout proposal,' he teased solemnly, 'would it?'

Kim managed a hollow little laugh while swallowing a lump of embarrassment in her throat. Although aware that he was merely teasing her, she was unable to appreciate the joke. 'I was only pointing out that if I can stand the heat other girls who've been born here can't have a great problem.'

'Even girls born here often find it too much for them.'

'I don't see why they should. If I . . .' aghast Kim broke off, realising she had been about to proclaim that if she'd loved a man and she was happily married to him she wouldn't mind where she lived. What would Garrick Lang have thought of her if she'd come out with that?

'You were saying?' she heard him prompting suavely, and her cheeks became scarlet as she suspected he had read her mind.

She was thankful that their arrival at Joe's door provided an excuse for not answering Garrick's question. 'It doesn't matter,' she didn't know her voice was thready with relief, 'I can manage now, Garrick, but it was nice of you to come with me.'

He accepted her rather breathless thanks but not his immediate dismissal. Abruptly he said, 'I'll see you inside.'

'There's no n . . .'

Kim felt herself lifted through the door by a strong, brawny arm which removed her breath before she could make a further protest. 'What did I tell you?' he snapped. 'Don't you ever listen!'

As the door closed behind them she wriggled from his hold. Jerkily she exclaimed, 'You make me feel about ten years old! Don't you want to tuck me in?'

'You put ideas in my head,' he taunted, 'and there are enough there already. Would you want a goodnight kiss as well?'

Cursing her wayward tongue which seemed determined to provoke him, Kim replied with a kind of forced flippancy. 'Don't you remember? I believe I had my goodnight kiss when we were out this morning.'

'That's Irish,' he grinned infuriatingly. 'My next line reads—"how could I ever forget!" but I'm more inclined to say, "I hope you don't imagine that was my best effort." '

Kim shrugged while two bright splashes of colour came and went under her smooth skin and she dropped her heavy, curling lashes for fear her eyes might reveal what she tried to hide by the indifferent movement of her shoulders. 'As a matter of fact,' she shrugged, 'I hadn't thought of it at all.'

'Strange,' he drawled sardonically, 'because I have.'

He had? A pulse did a dance in her throat, nearly choking her. 'I suppose it's easier for a girl to forget,' she faltered, wishing it was.

Twin sparks glinted in his eyes as he drawled, 'I must see that you don't forget so easily in future.'

She didn't have time to draw back, or even to guess what was happening, before his arms were around her and his hard mouth on hers. Unerringly, like an expert marksman, he immediately found his target, and if she had wondered secretly all afternoon what it would be like to be in his arms again, she didn't have to wonder any longer. As her lips were violently crushed apart, she realised their earlier entanglement had been but a brief salute compared with this. Yet when she tried to resist him, instead of struggling, she found herself clinging to him madly. As his demanding mouth plundered her own, her defences collapsed under waves of passion.

Trapped in a kind of nameless limbo, she could scarcely look at him as he lifted his head. 'Will that help your memory, do you think?' he asked mockingly.

Suddenly Kim was frightened and didn't want to get in any deeper. She couldn't match this man, for a start, and almost laughed at her own naïveté for ever daring to assume she might be able to. His arms were still around her, when she wriggled they merely tightened, but her freedom might be worth having to beg.

'Please let go of me,' she whispered.

'Not yet.' Speaking rather thickly, he again lowered his head, and she shivered as he pushed aside her long hair with one hand and pressed his mouth against her neck.

Whirled deeper into a wild storm of surging emotion, Kim wanted desperately to escape, but when she tried to move her legs threatened to give way under her, forcing her to reach out and grasp his waist for support. By the time his mouth returned to hers, her defences had crumbled and her senses were on fire. With a low groan he took her lips in a long searching kiss that took her breath away in its undisguised urgency.

Kim's heart felt as if it was about to burst. Nothing she had known before had prepared her for anything like this. Her veins were flowing with liquid fire, with waves of sensation running right through her. She would never have believed such feelings could exist inside herself. With an inarticulate little murmur she eased her arms from his waist to move them around his strong neck, letting her fingers curl their way through his dark, springy hair, clenching them into his scalp, unconsciously attempting to bring him even closer. There wasn't a thought in her head as she was swept by increasing desire, as Garrick Lang's firm mouth crushed and parted her own and his hands moved restlessly over her pliant body.

A car drawing up outside the door drove them apart. Almost immediately Joe charged in, followed by Rose. Joe's face fell when he saw Garrick. 'If I'd known you had company,' he said to Kim, 'I wouldn't have hurried back.'

Did he have to make it so obvious he suspected he had interrupted something? Kim bit her lip, hoping she didn't look as untidy as she felt and averted her eyes from Garrick's relaxed attempts to smooth out the mess she had made of his hair.

'You didn't have to hurry back,' she replied unevenly, her nerves suddenly strung tight. 'I wouldn't have taken any harm on my own.'

Rose smiled gently at her as she went towards the kitchen. 'I'll make some coffee,' she said.

Garrick said he wouldn't wait for any and left immediately after exchanging a brief word with Joe regarding something in the office. 'Goodnight, Kim,' he shot her a quick glance on his way out, 'see you in the morning.'

Joe rubbed his hands together, betraying that he was pleased about something. 'Good girl!' he chortled. 'I knew I could rely on you to keep your promise.'

'My promise? Oh, yes,' she replied absently, still too bemused by the events of the past hour to concentrate wholly on what Joe was saying.

The porch door banged, and as she started apprehensively, Joe said it was only the wind which had been rising as they came in. While he went to secure it, Kim slipped to the kitchen and told her aunt she didn't want any coffee either, then went to bed.

She rose early next morning, prepared to go to town, but on reaching Garrick's house she discovered that because Mrs Lang's shoulder had been so painful through the night, she was unable to even get out of bed. Kim didn't mind about not going to town, but she was sorry that Mrs Lang appeared to have suffered a relapse. When Garrick arrived, as she was leaving the house, she told him rather sharply that she thought he should send for the doctor.

'One can't be too careful. She may have broken something again. Mummy says, as we get older, our bones often get very brittle.'

'It's a pity girls didn't remember a few more of the things Mummy tells them,' he remarked, so pointedly she flushed.

'I'm talking about your mother, Garrick,' she said repressively.

'Well, I certainly pay heed to all the things she tells me,' he quipped outrageously. 'How otherwise would I still be unmarried?'

How otherwise, indeed! Kim had a sudden wild urge to tell him to go to hell. It didn't take a thought-reader to know he remained single by choice and that nothing anyone said or did would influence him one way or another! She didn't suppose he had listened to advice from his mother since he was knee-high in nappies. A fleeting amusement dispersed her irritation, curving her soft lips and making her eyes sparkle.

'Now what's amusing you?' he sighed in exasperation.

Unthinkingly she confessed, 'I was trying to imagine you in nappies.'

'Young lady,' he replied, dryly, 'I can't say I like the trend this conversation is taking. I'm assured I was irresistible even at that early age, but I thought we were talking about my mother.'

'I was! It was you—I mean . . .'

'What you mean is,' he interrupted smoothly, 'before you got embroiled in your womanly fantasising, you were busy telling me what to do about my mother.'

'No, I wasn't!' Kim exclaimed indignantly, 'I was merely making a suggestion, which not even you,' she added fiercely, 'can suggest is the same thing!'

He surprised her by putting a finger on her cheek, tracing it over her mouth to tilt up her chin. 'The doctor is already on his way,' he smiled, dropping a brief kiss on her startled lips as he left her.

Was it possible to both love and hate the same man? Kim wondered moodily as the door closed behind his tall figure. He always succeeded in rubbing her up the wrong way, yet she hated to think what her life would be like—what it was going to be like in six months time, without him? All the way home, as she returned to tell Rose she wouldn't now be going to town, she could feel the gentle touch of his lips on her own.

When Joe came in for lunch he told them the doctor had called and advised that Mrs Lang only required more rest and patience. He didn't think she had done a great deal of damage by using her arm too much too soon, but if it didn't improve he would have it X-rayed again. Later in the afternoon Kim called at the house to ask if Mrs Lang was feeling any better and Abby said much the same thing. She was keeping her mistress in her room and making her rest.

The following day Rose suggested to Kim that she might be able to give Abby a hand as she believed there was a party coming to look over some of Garrick's stud cattle and they would be here for lunch.

Willingly Kim changed into a clean blue gingham dress and set off. Abby was pleased to accept her offer of help, but just for the things Mrs Lang usually saw to.

'You can take her this cup of tea and have a word with her before you start,' she smiled. 'It will save my legs.'

Kim nodded and picked up the prepared tray as Abby quickly added another cup. With Abby's instructions she easily found Mrs Lang's bedroom. Mrs Lang wasn't in bed, she was sitting in her dressing-gown in a big chair near the window, and looked delighted to see Kim.

'Come and sit down, dear,' she said. 'I could do with a change of company. Abby and Garrick are dears, but I do get tired of their perpetual lecturing.'

A little later, when Kim asked if there was anything she could do for her, she said there certainly was. While she had managed to sort the pile of mail which had arrived for her yesterday, some of the letters had to be answered as soon as possible and her arm was still too sore to allow her to do it herself.

Kim promised she would help as soon as she had seen Abby and finished the jobs she wanted her to do. After laying the dining-room table, arranging fresh flowers and dusting the downstairs rooms, she collected a pad and some envelopes from Garrick's study and went back upstairs.

'I hope you remembered not to disturb anything and to close the study door?' Mrs Lang checked before beginning to dictate. 'If you didn't Garrick will have my head!'

'As the pad was exactly where you said it would be and the door is tightly closed, unless you mention it I don't suppose he'll ever know I've been,' Kim assured her.

They worked steadily for nearly two hours and Kim was glad of the experience she'd had in dealing with the shop correspondence. Mrs Lang was easy to work with, though, compared with her father, who was absentminded to a degree and usually managed to reduce their book-keeping system to an incredible muddle. Kim shuddered to think what would be waiting for her when she eventually returned.

Mrs Lang was delighted with her efforts. 'What beautiful handwriting—and how neat!' she exclaimed. 'My friends will all be wondering if I've got myself a secretary at last. I don't suppose,' she sighed wistfully, 'you'd care to help me, say once a week, while you're here?'

When Kim declared, perhaps rashly, that it would be a pleasure, Mrs Lang positively beamed. 'I won't let you forget,' she warned. 'Writing letters is a job I hate. The snag is I enjoy receiving them, which makes a reply essential. And then, as you can see, I do quite a lot of charity work and the paper work concerning that just has to be dealt with.'

Kim nodded sympathetically as she licked the stamps Mrs Lang gave her. 'Shall I leave these here with you?' she indicated the pile of completed letters.

'No, take them and put them on the hall table,' said Mrs Lang. 'Garrick will give them to the man who's coming from Perth. They'll get away quicker.'

Meeting Garrick in the hall, the letters in her hand,

Kim caught a flicker of coldness in his face, a moment before it was disguised by a faint smile. It was the same coldness she had thought she had noticed the previous morning, and she felt vaguely puzzled.

His words did nothing to settle her fleeting uneasiness. As his glance fell on the letters, his smile faded as he exclaimed grimly, 'Getting yourself established, I see?'

Kim's eyes betrayed a little of the hurt she felt at his sarcastic tones. This was the first time she had seen him since their meeting here yesterday, when he had kissed her. Could he be warning her, indirectly, not to take his kisses too seriously?

As if realising she was upset, Garrick sighed restively and laid a more friendly hand on her arm. 'You make me feel a brute,' he said wryly. 'I like seeing you around, but I've had a hell of a morning.'

'Didn't your buyer turn up?' she asked anxiously, forgetting his sharpness immediately.

'Oh yes,' he replied stonily, 'no problem there. In the lounge, waiting to be fed, are two very satisfied customers, and I've no doubt they'll feel even better after eating Abby's excellent lunch. But I wish I could say the same about my jackaroo.'

The jackaroo had been on holiday, so Kim hadn't met him, but she didn't waste time mentioning that. 'Why? Has something happened to him?'

'He just got on the wrong side of one of my Santa Gertrudis bulls,' he snapped, 'doing what he's been told a hundred times not to do. Fortunately Douglas Hamilton, the doc, managed to get here quickly, but I'm afraid it didn't make a good impression.'

'A good impression?' Kim felt bewildered.

'On the buyers, my dear child.' His voice rasped with impatience at having to explain something he obviously considered should have been clear to even an idiot! 'No one wants to buy an animal that looks in danger of going berserk.'

'But——' Kim stared at him for an interminable moment, her wide, confused eyes locked with his grey, angry ones, 'what about the—the jackaroo? Isn't he more important? What's going to happen to him?'

Garrick glared at her, as if he found the tense anxiety in her voice infuriating. 'I'll tell you what's going to happen to him, Blondie! As soon as he's able to travel, that's what he's going to do!'

'You—you mean you'd sack him? Just for making a mistake?'

The hand on her arm moved to the back of her head, giving her thick plait a sharp tug. 'It's not the first one he's made.'

'Don't do that!' she snapped.

'Pull your hair or dismiss the lad?'

'Both—I mean neither. Oh, for goodness' sake!' she stuttered, wondering how he could reduce her to such an infuriating muddle.

His shoulders lifted, his usual indication that the topic no longer interested him. As Kim's face grew red his relaxed. Indignantly, as she choked, she noticed his mouth even twitched slightly with amusement.

'Never try to speak,' he advised smoothly, 'until you're sure of what you want to say.' As Kim gazed at him mutinously, he let go of her hair to glance at his watch. 'I must be neglecting my guests,' he drawled. 'I expect,' his eyes went to the letters in her hand, 'my mother wants me to ask them to take those?'

'Oh, yes.' Kim handed them over.

'Quite a pile.' He weighed them lightly up and down. 'Did she commandeer your services?'

Kim smiled. 'I enjoy being useful.'

'Just as long as you don't overdo it. Give my mother an inch and she'll take all your time. You're here on holiday, remember.'

Because he sounded concerned for her, Kim felt warmly happy again. 'You don't have to worry over me,' she said softly. 'Brian's taking me riding this afternoon, after I finish helping Abby.'

About to pass her, Garrick suddenly paused. 'Did you say Brian?'

'Yes,' Kim faltered, recalling how Garrick had warned her to be wary of Brian and she hadn't really taken him seriously.

He didn't try to warn her again, he merely stated, 'Brian's going to be busy.'

'But he told me he had the afternoon off!' she exclaimed.

'Ah, but he hasn't.' Garrick's enigmatic stare dared her to deny his statement, but as her blue eyes clouded with disappointment he relented a little. 'If you want to go riding all that much, I'll take you myself, tomorrow.'

'But why?' she pleaded, wondering what she could say to Brian. She would much rather go out with Garrick, but it wouldn't be very kind to tell Brian that.

Garrick moved slightly, to cup her face with one hand, forcing her to look at him. She trembled and would have jerked away if his other hand hadn't fallen on her shoulder. Holding her still, he slowly and deliberately leaned forward. As she drew a sharp breath, he placed his mouth against hers, exploring its softness expertly before allowing the kiss to harden possessively to something much more demanding. He didn't release her until she began responding feverishly.

Then gently he broke from her, raising his dark head. 'Does that answer your question, Blondie? Did it never occur to you I might be jealous?'

As he left her, departing abruptly to entertain his guests, Kim turned unsteadily away, her heart singing. Yet as she helped Abby prepare the vegetables for serving with the succulent roast she was unable to rid herself of the notion that what seemed to be happening was just too wonderful to be true. There seemed no reason why Garrick shouldn't be attracted to her, as she was to him, but he didn't strike her as being a man who would be willing to show his feelings so quickly and so easily. She tried to dismiss the impression that he was acting deliberately, with something far from love on his mind. What if he hadn't love on his mind? Was it any crime for a man to seek the company of a pretty girl, especially if the girl proved she wasn't exactly unwilling?

Kim mashed potatoes until they were smooth and creamy, and sighed. All she had to do was avoid taking Garrick too seriously and enjoy herself! It was quite wrong to suspect he had some cruel ulterior motive in mind that might leave her stricken and brokenhearted!

As she came to the conclusion that at least he liked her, Kim's doubts faded and she felt happier. And her new optimism appeared justified when he came to the kitchen and asked if she would care to join the party for lunch. They were badly in need of a hostess. She was about to refuse when Abby urged her to accept, and to Kim's surprise she thoroughly enjoyed herself. The buyers were from a place called Esperance, south of Perth, and were involved in a huge project which included the development of over a million acres of land. She listened spellbound as they talked of their experiences, but they also wanted to know about life in the U.K., which they had visited but were never wholly familiar with.

Kim was surprised to find herself joining in the conversation easily if quietly, and if she sensed that the visitors had immediately taken to her, she was more thrilled by the glimmer of admiration she thought she caught in Garrick's eyes as they rested on her.

It was almost three when she managed to find Brian to tell him she couldn't go riding with him. Fearing she might hurt his feelings or make him angry by mentioning what Garrick had said, she mumbled something about being too tired after helping Abby. Silently she prayed that Abby wouldn't hear of it, or if she did that she would forgive her.

'How long has this been going on?' Brian was clearly

disgruntled. 'You aren't here to slave in the boss's house all day, you know.'

'Oh, I'm not—I don't,' Kim laughed, her face glowing. 'I don't mind helping out a bit, and actually it was your mother who suggested it, after I discovered Mrs Lang's arm was bad again.'

Brian stared at her suspiciously. 'Okay, if you say so,' he muttered. 'But you don't look very tired to me, and I'm not altogether sure I can trust you.' As Kim's cheeks flushed a guilty pink, his eyes narrowed even farther. 'You seem a secretive little thing. You didn't let on that Irene Ross had been here the other night.'

Kim thrust aside her involuntary indignation. Perhaps Brian had some justification in accusing her of keeping things to herself, but she had thought she was being discreet, rather than secretive. 'You were away, and she was Garrick's guest,' she replied awkwardly.

'She'd like to be more than that!' he retorted savagely.

Kim was too concerned with her own feelings to take much notice of Brian's tone. 'He has to marry some time, I suppose,' she sighed.

'Irene's been after him long enough.'

'But she married another man.'

Brian sneered. 'Only because she couldn't resist Jim Ross's money. Plus the fact that he was getting on in years and his heart wasn't very good. She probably imagined a sorrowing, wealthy widow might have more appeal for Garrick than a girl who couldn't get her man.'

While such reasoning was devious, Kim followed it. 'That's a hard thing to say about anyone, Brian!'

'The truth is often unpalatable, cousin,' he drawled.

Kim was still unconvinced. 'Mrs Ross is very goodlooking,' she frowned. 'I find it difficult to believe men don't find her attractive.'

'I didn't say that!' Brian paled in a way that puzzled

Kim. 'Her fault lies mostly in her one-track mind. She always wanted to be mistress here, and now she seems even more determined. She appears to imagine that Ross's money, plus Garrick, could be an unbeatable combination. Garrick wouldn't bite before, but now the money must be a great temptation. Like a lot of people, she's wondering how much longer he'll be able to resist it.'

As Brian kicked angrily at a lump of earth at his feet and walked abruptly away from her, Kim stared after him in bewilderment. Surely Garrick had enough money of his own to make Irene's relatively unimportant? Why did Brian seem to stress that the wealth was all on Irene's side? And why was he in such a bad mood about it?

Kim wasn't sure why she hadn't told her relatives about meeting Irene. It had, in fact, been on the tip of her tongue once or twice, when something—she didn't know what—had caused her to hesitate. She wondered, too, why they had never mentioned Irene to her, especially when she must be a very frequent visitor. It wasn't until a good while afterwards, when Joe failed to turn up for lunch one day and Rose sent Kim to see what was keeping him, that she suspected it was because they didn't like the girl.

As she approached the office she heard nothing to warn her of a quarrel taking place inside, and as she neared the door she was startled when Irene rushed out, her face flushed and looking furious. Having no wish to bump into her, in the mood she was obviously in, Kim retreated to the rear of the building, hoping Irene would soon be out of the way.

Kim had never intended eavesdropping, but unfortunately Irene must have stopped and gone back, because suddenly Kim heard her shouting shrilly.

'This isn't the last you'll hear of this, Joe Petre, let me tell you! Two years ago you thought you'd got rid of me, but I told you you were mistaken. You may think you have the upper hand, but you're going to be extremely sorry for some of the things you've said today! I may have been indiscreet with other men, but that doesn't mean Garrick's going to believe you. Believe me, as soon as I get back from Sydney you could be out of here—and fast!'

CHAPTER FIVE

JOE'S reply, if he made one, was lost in the noise of Irene's final departure. As she slammed the office door, Kim felt shaken by the venom in her voice and knew she hadn't been mistaken when she had sensed that the woman didn't like Joe. And the feeling must be mutual, if the one-sided conversation she had just overheard was anything to go by! Bleakly Kim wondered what it was all about. That Garrick was in some way involved seemed certain, but exactly how or why Kim wasn't prepared to guess.

She waited until the sound of Irene's car faded in the distance before she moved. Going into the office, she found Joe on his own and was amazed to see him as jaunty as ever. He made no mention of Irene, he didn't even say she had been.

'Aunt Rose sent me to tell you that lunch is ready,' she said, after he had bidden her unnecessarily to come in. 'Did you forget the time?'

'Tell your aunt I'll be there in about ten minutes,' he replied. 'I don't suppose there's anything getting cold.'

Kim was about to protest, but on taking a closer look at him she saw he was much more on edge than she had first thought. Deciding he probably needed time to pull himself together, she clamped down sharply on her growing curiosity and wandered back alone.

Later that afternoon she called to see the young jackaroo who had been injured. She had taken to visiting him when she had an hour to spare in order to cheer him up and she knew he enjoyed seeing her. He was being cared for by one of the stockmen's wives who had been a nurse before she had married. Normally he would have stayed at Garrick's house, but Garrick had decided Abby had enough to do looking after his mother.

Jon had cracked two ribs in his encounter with Garrick's bull, but he was sufficiently recovered to return home next day. His father had a sheep station in New South Wales.

'I think I'll stick to sheep after this,' he grinned, 'I always thought I fancied cattle, but not any more.'

Kim didn't know if Garrick knew of her visits. If he did he never mentioned it. It seemed unfortunate that he caught her coming from the Greens' bungalow, just as she was leaving for the last time.

He stared up at her as she stood on the high veranda steps outside the door, looking poised for flight, a startled, apprehensive expression in her face.

'So!' he exclaimed. 'If it isn't little Florence Nightingale herself! You do get around, don't you?'

Warily Kim stayed exactly where she was. It wasn't a question—it was more a statement with a sharp edge to it. She didn't like the hardness in his eyes, either, but she reminded herself that there were times when he regarded her more kindly.

'I don't believe you're as hard as you pretend to be,' she returned optimistically.

'Now what's that supposed to mean?' he enquired laconically.

'Nothing much.' She lifted her chin, defying him to wring a more satisfactory answer from her. 'I was just thinking aloud.'

'I'm sure your uncle told you to treat me with respect,' he said silkily.

'Oh yes!' Her blue eyes widened anxiously as she remembered, and she shivered to think she might be jeopardising Joe's chances of a good pension, though she found it difficult to believe that Garrick Lang would let a few sharp answers from a girl who was merely visiting influence any retirement arrangements he had made for his staff.

'When you've finished meditating, whether on Joe or that boy in there,' Garrick snapped, 'I'd appreciate your attention,' he paused, eyeing her grimly until her slightly scared nod assured him he had it, 'I have to go to Fitzroy Crossing. There's not much there, but I thought you might enjoy the drive. If you bring a costume we can stop and have a swim on our way back.'

'Oh, lovely!' Kim's nervousness disappeared as she agreed eagerly. 'But where is there to swim except your pool?'

'The river,' he replied briefly. 'There's not much water in it just now, but I know of at least one good spot.'

'Sounds wonderful,' she laughed, not bothering to hide her delight at the prospect of a cool dip. Glancing down at her jeans, she asked doubtfully, 'While I'm getting my costume should I change?'

'No, come as you are. But you'd better tell Rose where you're going,' he called after her as she ran past him.

Ten minutes later they set off. With Garrick beside her, Kim found she was looking forward to the trip immensely, although she had been quite content to stay on Coolarie until now.

'Everything okay?' he asked, climbing into the Range-Rover after her and closing the door.

'It seems so.' She turned a glowing face towards him. 'Aunt Rose says I should get safely back, as you're a good driver.'

'Did she indeed!' as he drove away he turned his dark head and caught her teasing laughter. 'What she doesn't know is that I'm going to make you drive back. I want to see how competent you are before I allow you out with Rose and my mother.'

So he wasn't taking her just for the pleasure of her company. Pain brought instant resentment, and she was about to exclaim sharply that she was wholly competent when she suddenly changed her mind. The part of the road they were travelling on at the moment was little more than an unsurfaced track. Naturally Garrick would want to take reasonable precautions to ensure the safety of his mother. She closed her mouth tightly before a word of indignation could escape.

'What, no comeback?' Garrick's eyebrows quirked mockingly.

'Plenty,' Kim smiled wryly. 'It was when I was counting ten . . .'

'That you realised I was talking sense?' he finished for her.

'Well, it is your country . . .' she shrugged.

He changed gear with a slight jerk which surprised her. 'Ever thought of making it yours?'

A dust cloud swirled up behind them. Kim drew a sharp breath. 'I've only been here a few weeks,' she said stiffly.

'So you have,' he agreed, as if her reply was entirely sensible. 'My, how time flies! It seems more like a few years!'

His voice was full of sarcasm, and it puzzled her—as did his sudden swings from friendliness to what she could only describe as leashed anger. She fell silent, contenting herself with occasional glimpses of his strong profile as he concentrated on the road. She loved it when his face softened, but when it hardened, as if from unpalatable thoughts, she looked at the scenery.

The silence lasted so long, she almost jumped when Garrick broke it abruptly. 'Do you know what your uncle said to Irene to make her leave in such a hurry? We were expecting her to lunch.'

Kim shrugged. 'Someone said they'd seen you near the office when she hurried out.'

'Yes. So what?' Kim didn't like the feeling of being trapped. 'If you know so much how is it no one told you I'd been sent to find Uncle Joe for his lunch? I realise he and Mrs Ross were having a quarrel, but I just caught the end of it. I've no idea what it was about. Does it matter?' she asked more belligerently, knowing nicely it might be futile to hope for a straightforward answer to that!

'Not really,' he angered her by confirming her suspicions. 'We'd better drop the subject,' he said smoothly. 'I don't want to spoil your day.'

As he glanced at her closely, she felt like telling him he had already spoiled it! Subjected to his intent scrutiny, she squirmed and her cheeks went pink, which made her mad again as she was aware he might mistake this for a sign of guilt and be convinced she was withholding something.

She was more than relieved when, minutes later, they arrived at Fitzroy Crossing and her spirits rose as she gazed around with eager curiosity. She didn't think it was any larger than an English village, certainly not as pretty, but still it looked interesting.

Garrick parked near the end of the street, outside a cluster of buildings. 'If you want anything,' he said, 'there's the store and the post office. I'll give you half an hour.'

Kim brushed a few curling strands of fair hair from off her face as she hopped alongside him down the sidewalk. 'I should have asked your mother if she was short of anything.'

Glancing down into her ruefully anxious eyes, he placed a lean hand on her arm to steady her. 'I told her I was coming in, but she didn't want anything. She's going to Perth tomorrow for a week or two and can get all she needs there.'

'G—going to Perth?' Kim's dewy lips parted in astonishment.

'I'd close your mouth, darling, unless you want me to do it for you,' he taunted. 'As it is, you're attracting enough attention.'

'All right!' she muttered mutinously, as his hand tightened on her arm, drawing her close threateningly, 'So, I'm surprised. What else would you expect me to be, after she's been so ill?'

'Not so ill.' His arm clipped around her shoulders,

drawing her flying footsteps to a halt as he paused. 'It's only her shoulder, the condition of which she's been crafty enough to exaggerate a little in order to secure your expert secretarial services. Before she hurt herself again, she had already made arrangements to stay with a friend in Perth and combine her visit with the excellent physiotherapy treatment available there. By going tomorrow she's merely following up postponed plans.'

'I see . . .'

Garrick's brawny arm was burning a brand across her back. 'No, you don't.' His breath was warm on her face as he leaned anxiously nearer. 'You're feeling hurt.'

If she was, it was fast disappearing under something much stronger. 'I've no right to feel hurt,' she whispered honestly.

He regarded her pale cheeks steadily. 'The doc only gave his permission for her to travel this morning. She hasn't seen you since, but I know she intends to explain.'

'She doesn't have to.' Kim forced herself to pull firmly away from him before the churning emotions inside her took over and she found herself clinging to him instead. 'After all, I'm not one of the family.'

'Not yet,' he replied, staring at her for a moment before leaving her, his eyes smouldering.

Whatever did he mean by that? Kim's heart turned somersaults while her pulse raced with a kind of aching excitement as she watched his tall figure striding from her down the street. Could it be that he was falling in love with her? And thinking seriously of asking her to be his wife? If ever he did, would she be able to refuse him? Would she even want to refuse him, suspecting as she did that she loved him more than she had ever loved anyone in her life?

With the heat dancing all around her, Kim felt like dancing herself as she walked along. Her thoughts were so buoyant she frequently imagined she was walking on air and was unable to concentrate on what she was doing. Consequently she didn't buy much, just a small present for Rose and a few toiletries for herself. By the time she met Garrick again she was hot and thirsty but dreamily content.

'You don't appear to have bought much, but you seem happy enough,' he observed shrewdly.

His formal manner caused Kim to pull herself together. Whatever happened he mustn't be allowed to guess the rather foolish direction her thoughts had taken during the past half hour. His grey eyes were so coolly aloof that she must have been crazy to think he might be coming to care for her!

'To tell you the truth,' she sighed, 'the one thing I really wanted I couldn't find—a long, cool drink.'

'I can help you there.' His stern features relaxed in a grin as he took her arm. 'We'll visit the hotel before making our way to the river. I could do with something myself.'

'At home we aren't allowed to drink and drive,' she teased, as inside the hotel Garrick ordered lemonade for her and a large whisky for himself.

His mouth quirked mockingly as he steered her over to a quiet corner. 'I usually stick to the same rules myself,' he retorted suavely. 'Why do you imagine I ordered you lemonade? You're the one who's driving back, remember?'

She couldn't help pulling a rueful face at him. 'You never overlook a thing, do you?'

'I try not to,' he drawled sardonically, 'otherwise I might easily be outwitted by a charming but very devious young lady from another planet.'

'Ha, ha!' she muttered, trying to sound more amused than she felt, as incredibly all her instincts warned her Garrick wasn't entirely joking.

The hotel was pleasant and comfortable and Garrick assured her the food was good. 'Do many tourists get as far as this?' she asked, changing the subject to something less personal.

'Quite a few.' He watched her lazily as he savoured his drink. 'The Kimberley region is quite famous, you know. In the north we have the Ord Dam, the Ord River irrigation scheme which flooded the Argyle station of the famous Durack family—you've probably read some of Mary Durack's books? Then apart from the beef industry, we have schemes for cotton and rice and various other crops. And, of course, there's the mining. The Pilbara is probably the biggest high-grade iron ore zone in the world. They have a lot of that, too, on the islands across the Yampi Sound. I'll have to take you to the islands one day. They form part of the Buccaneer Archipelago and they're very beautiful.'

'Hasn't the mining spoiled them?' Kim asked.

'No,' he said, 'not at all.'

This promise, if that was what it was, of things to come, caused Kim to begin wondering again, despite herself, about Garrick's intentions. And because the warmth in his eyes as they rested on her encouraged the notion that he was falling in love with her, she was relieved when he rose to his feet, declaring if they wanted a swim they had better be going.

'You ought to have been here in September,' he said as they wandered outside again. 'We have picnic races and people come from all over the Kimberley. You would have had fun.'

There it was again, she thought, the slight cynicism which kept cropping up, putting her on edge, destroying her confidence. She was still tense when they reached the spot where the Range Rover was parked.

'Ever driven one before?' Garrick asked abruptly.

Kim's chin came up at his doubtful tones, but her heart sank in the other direction. This wasn't a moment for confession, though, she had to make a stand somewhere!

'I've driven plenty of large vehicles,' she replied cooly. And so she had! Wasn't her father always buying an old truck or car of some sort to transport his various bargains home from scattered salerooms and country houses? They might never have risen to a Range-Rover; they could never have afforded one like Garrick's, which was still a fairly new baby from the looks of it. Some baby! Kim swallowed, trying to estimate the cost of it, the cost of repairs should she do any damage.

'I know it's beautiful,' Garrick remarked dryly, 'but we don't have time to stand admiring it all day. Get in and get cracking!'

Did he have to order her around so tersely? It wasn't as if she worked for him! 'Have you no patience?' she snapped, forgetting all about loving him.

'Go ahead,' he drawled, leaning back in his seat, folding his arms idly as she furtively scanned the dashboard. 'Don't mind me. Concentrate on your audience out there. They surely appreciate the opportunity to study a girl with a figure like yours.'

As she turned her head to glare at him, her cheeks flushed to find his gaze deliberately slanted on her breasts. A hot wave of something swept over her, nearly swamping her.

'Do you mind!' she gritted between clenched teeth. 'I realise my tee-shirt is a little tight, but you said not to change.'

'Oh,' his mouth quirked insolently without averting his eyes, 'I like a pair of good . . .'

'Will you shut up!' she half screeched, locating the brake at exactly the same moment as she switched the ignition and found the accelerator. As she let go of everything at once, except for her right foot which she fiercely pressed to the floor, the vehicle appeared to take off in a series of high leaps.

'God almighty!' Garrick yelled, as he was jerked forwards and backwards in quick and painful succession at least three times before he managed to apply the handbrake. 'What the hell do you think you're doing?'

The derisory cheers which they had began leaving

behind caught up, but the scattering of faces that peered in on them were no longer solemnly curious but openly grinning and loud with advice.

'Start it up again!' Garrick ordered grimly, his temper obviously at boiling point as she turned to him appealingly. 'No, I'm not driving! Stay right where you are. Of all the dumb sheilas! Now your gears—a little more acceleration, then your brake. Take—your—foot—off—the—brake!'

Amazingly, seeing how Kim was visibly shaking and merely obeying automatically, the Range-Rover glided smoothly away. Perhaps glide wasn't exactly the right word, but it was a vast improvement on her first attempt.

'Change up!' Garrick snapped, just as she was beginning to relax.

'Don't shout at me, you great bully!' she shouted back. 'I was going to. The trouble with you, you're always in too great a hurry!'

'Not that much of a hurry!' he retorted sourly as she crashed through the gears and their speed shot up to seventy. 'I'd like to live a little longer, if you don't mind!' Kim calmed down to a sedate thirty. 'You're a rotten driver,' he groaned, rubbing his head.

'Thank you!' she returned as coldly. 'So what? I'm a rotten tennis player, swimmer and horsewoman. I don't expect to be good at much.'

'Oh no!' he drew a loud, steadying breath. 'First you try to kill me, now I'm being treated to an overdose of inferiority complex. There's nothing wrong with your tennis or swimming or riding,' he snapped. 'You lack experience, that's all.'

'Oh, good!' she retorted dryly, flinging him a sarcastic glance. 'And where do I get that? Fairies, I suppose?'

'From me,' he replied, meeting her dark glance without moving a muscle. 'You'll be average to good before I'm through with you, and that's all you need be. That way you'll be far more popular than the girl who wins every time.'

Feeling somewhat chastened, she managed to mutter, 'I've never been that ambitious.'

'Furthermore,' he added, as her eyes clouded doubtfully, 'if I lost my temper back there, don't you think you deserved it?'

'Yes,' she whispered, knowing he was right. 'I'm sorry. If your mother or Aunt Rose had been with me they could have had a bad fright.'

'Anyone not so tough as I am,' he agreed dryly.

When she bit her lip and went pale as the remorse she felt threatened to overwhelm her, he smiled forgivingly. 'Come on, let's find that spot in the river, then we can at least begin your swimming lessons.'

The Fitzroy river in the Wet, from December to March, was usually a raging torrent, but during the dry season it became a string of picturesque pools. Some were permanent waterholes, attracting a great variety of fish and wild life. Near Fitzroy Crossing, Garrick had shown her one of the best known of these, Geikie Gorge, probably one of the most colourful and spectacular of all the accessible river gorges in Northern Australia, except, he thought, the Katherine River one in the Northern Territory.

Kim had been impressed by the Geikie Gorge, with its wonderful limestone cliffs, and had wanted to swim there until Garrick had mentioned that it was probably full of sharks and sawfish and freshwater crocodiles. Although he had assured her that the Johnson crocodile is a fish eater and, unlike the saltwater crocodile, which lives near the mouth of all Kimberley rivers, has never been known to attack man, she refused to stay.

'I've no desire to make a dinner for a ravenous monster like that!' she declared nervously.

'Do you think one might fancy you?' Garrick teased.

'There's no accounting for taste,' she retorted, driving on determinedly.

An hour later they came to a pool which Garrick solemnly promised wasn't large enough to harbour any lethal predators. 'You can change in here,' he said, as she stopped the Range-Rover at a spot he indicated. 'Unless you prefer those bushes over there?'

'No, I'd rather stay where I am.' She patently weighed the disadvantages of uncurtained windows against those of prickly cactus and perhaps snakes.

He grinned, moving away after collecting a pair of faded blue shorts from one of the seats. Imagining he was going to use the bushes, Kim followed his progress absently with her eyes as he walked along the side of the gorge. Pausing on the rock face, he began taking off his shirt. She started in alarm as she soon realised this wasn't all he intended to remove, in full view of anyone who happened to be looking. His shoes came next, then his belt, and she could almost hear the rasp of his zip.

His pants followed, and, as they came down, exposing more of his powerful body, she realised with startled apprehension that she was staring. Quickly directing her transfixed gaze elsewhere, she feverishly dealt with her own clothing. When her hands fumbled she blamed the tension of the drive, rather than the sight of Garrick's bare, muscled frame. It took her so long to put on her bikini that before she was ready he was shouting for her to hurry up.

When she emerged from the shelter of the car, he barely glanced at her. As she walked towards him over the hot rocks, he stepped to the edge of one and dived off. Kim shivered, although she was hot and sticky and longed above all things to go in after him. It must be ridiculous to feel she might be diving into more than deep water.

The pool was only about twenty yards across, yet she could see no sign of him. Then he emerged, his dark hair dripping wet, his broad shoulders square and gleaming like satin. As he stared at her she drew a sharp breath, feeling almost as naked as he had been a few minutes ago.

'Come on in. What are you waiting for?' he called.

'Maybe I'm still nervous!' she called back.

'Do I look like a croc?' he sighed impatiently. 'I can assure you if there was anything man-eating in here they'd have had me by now. I've been right along the bottom.'

How could she tell him she was more nervous of him than any crocodile?

'If you don't move I'm coming to get you,' he threatened.

Fearing he might be as good as his word, Kim slanted her arms and dived off the edge with more haste than grace. The temperature of the water was low enough to cool her heated skin, she thought it was delicious. Swiftly it swept away the tensions of the afternoon and she came up spluttering but laughing.

'That was wonderful!' she cried, rubbing the water from out her eyes to ensure it was Garrick and not one of the massive hulks of rock she was speaking to.

'You took your time,' he said softly as she paddled idly beside him.

She nodded, swimming away from him towards the other side of the pool and the small, stony beach she saw there. The water was deep and clear, she could see the floor of the pool a long way down. She swam several more yards before her feet touched the bottom near the sandy shore, but she was too conscious of the brevity of her costume to leave the protection of the water entirely.

Garrick came up behind her, water clinging to the matted hair on his chest. Her eyes flickered as they slowly met his, shaken by what seemed a moment of complete intimacy. He smiled and she felt she was blushing all over.

Blindly she turned, wading ashore, and heard him following, his heavier footsteps making crunching noises on the gravel. The beach was backed by high cliffs, there was nowhere to go. Leaving the water had been a mistake. In it only her head and shoulders had been visible, but here there was nothing to veil her from his prolonged scrutiny. And scrutinise her he did, without apology. His eyes strayed across her firm, high curves, her gently rounded belly, her taut thighs and long slim legs, until all her tension returned again. She felt her nerves jumping as his gaze came back to her face. He watched closely as, reduced to a state of scarcely knowing what she was doing, she lifted the heavy strands of her honey-coloured hair and began dragging them around to the nape of her neck.

'Don't do that,' his hand reached out to hold hers still, but he spoke almost tenderly. 'I like seeing it floating behind you in the water. You make a wonderful mermaid.'

Kim laughed, attempting to ease the constriction inside her rather than because she was very amused by what he said. Very carefully she edged from his grip and managed to say casually, 'It might be fabulous to be a mermaid in these pools. Everything's fantastic. I'd like to explore that waterfall over there. Any objections?'

'It should be safe enough,' he smiled, 'if that's what you're asking?'

As his brows tilted enquiringly and his eyes returned to study her again, she knew if she didn't escape she might lose all desire to do so. Swiftly she struck out for the north end of the escarpment, where the water tumbled twenty feet from the river above. Garrick followed, keeping behind her when he could easily have overtaken her. The distance was farther than she had judged, and before she reached the falls she was breathless, but the spray falling on her upturned face was delightful and well worth swimming the extra distance for.

Lowering her head, she trod water, wondering where Garrick had got to, waiting for him. She wished she had somewhere to sit. As the undercurrents buffeted her, she felt like a rubber ball bouncing up and down. Garrick had left her to circle the pool, getting rid of leashed energy. She liked watching his long, powerful strokes, the way his big body cleaved smoothly through the water. She noticed he scarcely disturbed a ripple on the surface.

He disappeared, and she wished he wouldn't play such tricks on her—if that was what he was doing. Minutes later, when he bobbed up beside her, it was too late to hide the apprehension in her face.

'For goodness' sake!' she cried, trying to disguise her anxiety with anger. 'Must you do that? What a fright you gave me!'

His eyes glinted mockingly. 'I enjoy frightening you. You react so beautifully.'

'Beast!' she choked, really amazed that he could be so heartless and hoping he wouldn't notice her eyes were damp with unexpected tears.

He did notice, but to her hurt astonishment with amusement rather than remorse. 'Come here,' he teased, 'and I'll kiss you better.'

'No!' As his arm shot out she dodged, unfortunately sinking like a stone as she moved too quickly and her limited experience let her down. On her way to the bottom she swallowed water because, as usual, she forgot to close her mouth. Frantically she thrashed out for anything that might save her, and the first thing she found was one of Garrick's well muscled legs.

Immediately his arms went around her as he recognised she needed help. Lifting her against his rock-hard body, he swiftly brought her upright again. The breath knocked out of her, she clung to him, her arms tightly around his neck.

'All right?' he asked.

How many times, she wondered dazedly, had he asked her that before? 'Yes,' she whispered, while not feeling brave enough to let go of him. Floating against him, she relied on him to support her. As she slowly regained her breath she felt the first prickle of awareness running through her from being so near him. When the water, ebbing between them, threatened to drive them apart, his arms tightened. As this brought her closer again and her thinly covered breasts rubbed against his broad, hair-covered chest, the sensual feeling this evoked made her gasp. And Garrick increased the erotic sensation by holding her firmly to the lower part of his body.

He moved slightly, his thighs thrusting against hers and away again, carrying her towards a rocky ledge behind the falls. She was sure that half the waves must be caused by the thudding of her heart. A pulse beat rapidly in her throat and he watched it intently. Then she trembled violently as his hands loosened the tie at the back of her bikini and unhooked the top, releasing it so that it floated gently away.

Kim knew she should be furious, but so many other emotions were sweeping through her there seemed no room for anger. Garrick's eyes scanned her pale features and one hand cupped her chin, forcing her to look at him. As she did, she thought he was trying to dissect her very soul.

Carefully he lifted her to the ledge, hauling himself out of the water to lie down beside her. They were in a wide alcove between the back of the falls and the cliff face, which was quite dry apart from some odd drops of water. Kim didn't struggle. If she had wanted to she didn't know where she would have found the strength, as Garrick's nearness seemed to be taking every bit of it from her shaking limbs.

'This is crazy,' he muttered, as if to himself.

'I know,' she murmured back, ashamed of the eagerness in her voice but unable to prevent herself from loving him desperately.

With a groan he pulled her to him, parting her mouth with the force of his own, and her arms slid compulsively around his neck again. As she was crushed against the hard warmth of his body, she felt herself succumbing to the dizzying appeal of his potent virility. It hit her in waves and she was helpless to stop him as he bent his head to kiss the deep hollow between her breasts.

His mouth moved over her nakedness with a maddening slowness. He seemed to be savouring every inch of her, turning the smouldering heat in her flesh to leaping flames of desire. She began kissing him back and there was a deep sound of satisfaction in his throat as he swiftly aroused her passionate responses. She whimpered with a tingling pleasure as his mouth moved sensually across her breast, capturing one erect nipple.

There was a tremor in his hands as they removed the bottom half of her bikini, then gently caressed her bareness. With a smothered exclamation he lay on top of her, but just as swiftly rolled off.

'Help me,' he whispered thickly, trying to get rid of his own wet shorts. Blindly Kim raised herself on one elbow to free the top button, beyond caring any more about what he wanted to do to her. She had never dreamed that a man's hands and mouth could evoke such sensations, and she was beyond denying them.

Becoming as impatient with her fumbling fingers as he had been with his own, Garrick jerked savagely from her to complete the operation himself. Unfortunately the sudden movement brought him dangerously near the outside ledge, and as Kim, caught off guard, fell against him, she inadvertently pushed him over the edge back in the water.

Startled, she heard the heavy splash and found herself alone in the echoing tunnel—alone and painfully tormented, both by her unsatisfied desires and the doubts which began raining down on her like the drops of water which descended from the falls on her despairing head.

A few moments later, when she had had time to briefly pull herself together, Garrick's hand appeared through the curtain of cascading water. To her astonishment he was dangling her bikini top, and as he let go of it, it fell by her side.

As she grabbed it weakly, he withdrew, but though she could no longer see him, she heard his voice.

'You'd better get dressed, Blondie,' he called harshly. 'And be as quick as you like—it's time to leave. Swim over to me when you're ready.'

Kim drew a quick breath, wondering anxiously why he should sound so curt. Could he have hurt himself when he had fallen over the ledge? 'Are you all right?' she asked unsteadily.

'Yes,' he grated mockingly, 'you don't have to worry on my account. There's nothing like a cold dip for bringing a man to his senses!'

CHAPTER SIX

GARRICK drove back to Coolarie. He didn't ask how she felt or if she wanted to drive. He waited until she had dressed, then took one look at her pale, strained face and didn't look again. At the homestead, when he dropped her off with a casual, 'See you tomorrow,' he didn't even wait until she walked away.

Joe was in a good mood, and wanted to know what had kept them so late.

'We went swimming,' Kim replied without thinking.

'Swimming?' He sounded surprised. 'Where?'

Coming out of the trance she seemed to have been in since Garrick kissed her, Kim became aware that she was being questioned. 'In the pool, in the river,' she answered briefly, regretting now that she'd ever mentioned it.

'Humm,' Joe glanced at her sharply, 'I've never known Garrick take a girl there before. When he has company he usually sticks to the pool at the house.'

'You can't know what he's doing all the time!' she retorted, trying to be patient.

'I've a good idea what goes on when he's here,' Joe boasted, making Kim shiver. 'I have my—er—sources of information, shall we say.'

Kim stared at him, feeling a surge of repugnance which she quickly dispersed. After all, Joe was her uncle. She only hoped whoever it was who supplied him with information hadn't been near the river today. 'Where's Aunt Rose?' she asked quickly, changing the subject.

Joe wasn't offended by Kim's obvious reluctance to discuss her afternoon. Carefully he lit a cigar, drawing on it with lazy satisfaction. 'She's gone to see one of

95

the men's wives about something. I believe she said your supper's in the oven.'

Kim couldn't face the rather gluey-looking casserole she found, so she made herself some cocoa and a sandwich instead and carried it to bed, hoping her aunt would forgive her. Joe had looked disappointed when she bade him a hurried goodnight, but not altogether despondent. Kim supposed she should forgive him for seeming over-curious about everything, but there were limits! For his sake she prayed Garrick never found out he was being watched so closely, for if he did she was sure he might dismiss Joe and his family immediately, despite the fact that they were related.

It was this ruthless streak in Garrick which made Kim apprehensive on her own account. His mood, when they had parted earlier, had been incomprehensible but she had realised he was angry—that puzzling anger which always returned, she thought unhappily, as she undressed.

It was easy to climb into bed but not so easy to fall asleep, not with thoughts buzzing round in her head until it began aching. She was aware that she had made a fool of herself at the pool. She still couldn't think of it without trembling, and went cold when she recalled the scorn in Garrick's eyes when she had eventually rejoined him beside the Range Rover.

His opinion of her had been obvious, but if he did think the worst of her could she blame him? Hadn't she been startled herself by the depth of her own response to his intense assault on her emotions? She had been lost as the passionate clamourings of her body had taken complete control of her mind.

A frown creased her smooth brow and again she shivered. If Garrick had wanted to possess her there was nothing she could have done to stop him, and he must have guessed how she had felt. And if she had wanted him he had wanted her—of that she felt pretty certain. Inexperienced as she was, she had sensed the need in his searching, passionate kisses and in his body which he had allowed to reveal quite blatantly the extent to which he had been aroused.

Yet he hadn't returned to finish what he had so ruthlessly begun. She didn't even know whether he had slipped back into the pool by accident or design. The more Kim thought of it, the more she became convinced that he had allowed a fundamental respect for her innocence to influence him against going any farther. He must love her a little, she reasoned almost tearfully, to have been able to subdue the force of his own strong desires sufficiently to have allowed him to leave her before anything drastic had happened.

Joe came early for his breakfast next morning. 'If you've finished yours,' he said to Kim, 'Garrick would like to see you in his office.'

Kim drank the last of her coffee with a gulp. 'Have you any idea what about?' she asked cautiously.

'No, I haven't,' Joe replied, 'but if you'd like me to guess, he probably wants you to go somewhere with him.'

Kim didn't think so, not so soon, anyway, after yesterday. 'It could be about his mother,' she said. Collecting her hat, she called to Rose that she wouldn't be long.

Garrick was waiting for her, sitting on the edge of the big desk, reading a printed form. When Kim arrived he laid it down and gave her his full attention.

'Are you all right?' he enquired suddenly, surprising her.

She glanced at him quickly, hating the colour that rushed to her cheeks as she met his narrowed eyes. She could have done without his rather belated enquiry, she thought resentfully. Wasn't she trying to forget yesterday ever happened? Did he have to remind her? 'Yes,' she replied shortly, 'I feel quite all right, thank you.'

He sighed, his glance trained on her small, mutinous face, but he didn't pursue the matter. 'I wanted a word with you, Kim, before you saw my mother. At least, I was presuming that you'd be calling to see her.'

Kim nodded eagerly, forgetting her own problems. 'I was going to try and catch her before she left. Are you taking her to Perth?'

'No, I'm only taking her as far as Derby. It's something I often do when she wants to go away. She's going to ask if you'll come with us and return with me tomorrow. As she's had a bad night, I wanted to make sure you wouldn't refuse.'

'You mean you won't let me?'

'If you choose to put it that way—no.'

Kim's eyes widened. Garrick wasn't her employer, yet he took a delight in ordering her around! If it hadn't been for his mother, whom she liked very much, she would tell him exactly where to go to!

Hiding her indignation, she said slowly. 'I'd do any-thing for your mother, Garrick, you know that, but are you sure she wants me? Wouldn't she rather have someone else to assist her? Someone she knows better, like—well, Mrs Ross, for instance . . .?'

'Kim,' Garrick broke in dryly, 'whether you take it as a compliment or not, it's you she wants. And Irene has gone to Sydney for a few weeks, so it's no use thinking of her. Now, how about it? I haven't all day and I'd like this settled. With or without you, we leave in a few hours, and I've a lot to do before then.'

'I'd love to go,' Kim suddenly gave in willingly, 'if you think I can manage. You realise I'm not a trained nurse?'

'She doesn't need a nurse.' Garrick's eyes roved over her slender figure and he spoke almost absently. 'She may require help tonight, in the hotel, but no actual nursing. In the morning we put her on a plane for Perth where her friend will meet her. She'll be looked after all the way.'

Garrick was clearly in a hurry to be gone, but Kim insisted. 'You should have let her ask me herself. Why didn't you?'

'Because, my dear girl,' he grated, 'I wasn't sure how

you'd be feeling this morning and I didn't want her upset. I have enough on my mind without that.'

So when he'd asked solicitously if she was all right, his concern had really been for himself! Then, as he left the desk and paused by her side on his way to the door, her anger suddenly evaporated. Garrick was a busy man, she couldn't expect him to be patient all the time. 'Of course I won't refuse,' she smiled up at him, her eyes meeting his warmly. 'I'll go now and help your mother all I can. We'll be ready when you are.'

Kim's previous visit to Derby had lasted only for as long as it had taken to get from one plane to another. On this trip she doubted if she would see much more of the town as they had been late in leaving and it was after six in the evening before they arrived. They had travelled in Garrick's small plane. They could have made the journey by road, but Garrick couldn't spare the time and Mrs Lang had feared that any jolting might upset her shoulder.

The hotel was comfortable and they dined early. The Langs were obviously well known and respected and were given the best the hotel had to offer. Garrick was attentive and Kim enjoyed her meal very much, but immediately afterwards he disappeared to see a friend and business colleague.

'He's always mixing business with pleasure,' his mother sighed, as Kim helped her to her room. 'I won't wait up for him as one never knows what time he'll be back. I should go to bed too, my dear, if I were you,' she advised as Kim left her.

So much for her pretty dress and the extra care she had taken with her make-up! Kim stared at her image in the mirror, in the privacy of her bedroom, with something near disgust. 'You didn't help much,' she spoke aloud, grimacing wryly. Garrick had glanced at her often enough during dinner, but there had been little in his eyes that she could see, apart from a gleam of sardonic humour. It had seemed almost as if he'd been laughing at her, or at something he believed she hoped to achieve. She wished she had been able to look at him as indifferently. She wished she could stop thinking of Garrick and his kisses, the taste of his lips, warm and sweet on her mouth. Why couldn't she forget about his heavy, slippery body, the burning sensation of their two bodies pressed passionately together—of how much he had wanted her under the waterfall? She had wanted him too, as desperately as she had longed to hear him say he loved her, but instead he had left her. He hadn't even spared her a kind word afterwards, and the more she thought of it, the more she just wanted to die.

Mrs Lang's plane left the next afternoon. She had decided it would be wiser to wait rather than go to Perth in the morning, in order to give herself time to recover from the first stage of her journey.

'I'm a terrible traveller,' she said laughingly to Kim over breakfast, 'even when I'm a hundred per cent fit. I don't know what I shall do when Garrick marries, if his wife won't put up with me.'

'Oh, I'm sure any girl would love having you for a mother-in-law,' Kim laughed back. 'I know I should!'

Garrick's head jerked sharply from his newspaper, and Kim was overcome by confusion. She tried to explain that she had spoken without thinking, but the words couldn't get past the tight embarrassment in her throat. She was grateful to Mrs Lang for smoothing what might have been an awkward moment by exclaiming cheerfully.

'You're so good for my morale, Kim! You spoil me by saying such nice things. Now I must go shopping and find something for Mary.'

Mary was the friend she would be staying with, and she spent a good part of the morning finding something suitable. Garrick had gone off again on business, leaving the two women free to wander alone. As they were leaving the store where Mrs Lang had found exactly what she was looking for, Kim's eyes widened as she paused compulsively to admire a model dress on a stand. It was an evening dress in blue chiffon, sleeveless with glittering insets of silver diamanté decorating the low neckline and wide belt. Beside it was another in green silk taffeta, but she liked the blue one best.

'How lovely!' she breathed.

'Just right for you, I should think,' said Mrs Lang.

Kim had forgotten her. 'True,' she smiled ruefully, 'but I don't really need a dress like that.'

'Every girl needs a dress like that!' Mrs Lang was already beckoning imperiously to the saleswoman. 'If it fits, Kim, I'm going to buy it for you. Haven't I been racking my brains this past hour, wondering just what you would like?'

'But I don't want anything!' With increasing agitation, Kim watched as the woman ascertained that the dress was exactly her size. 'Oh, please, Mrs Lang!' she protested helplessly.

'Now you listen to me, Kim,' Mrs Lang said aggressively. 'You've done me a favour by coming with me to Derby. You must allow me to do something for you.'

The dress was as gorgeous on Kim as it had looked on the stand. It only required to be taken in a little at the waist as Kim was so slender. The shop promised this could easily be done by mid-afternoon.

'We'll take it,' Mrs Lang swept aside another spate of protests from Kim. 'Garrick won't mind waiting a few minutes, you'll see.'

Unfortunately they had to wait much longer than a few minutes, and Garrick was furious. After his mother had gone he berated Kim angrily for forgetting he was in a hurry. 'You didn't have to persuade my mother into buying you a new dress,' he snapped, 'I was going to give you a cheque.'

His disparaging tone left her feeling wholly insulted. Her blue eyes flashed as they reflected her feelings. 'I didn't ask your mother to buy me anything,' she retorted icily. 'She insisted, and short of being rude I couldn't stop her.'

Suddenly Garrick smiled smoothly. 'I expect she considered, as my future wife, you needed something extra?'

Kim didn't notice the silky tones. For a moment she thought he was proposing, and a radiant glow lit her eyes. Wordlessly, not caring what her face revealed, she stepped nearer, only to halt with a jerk as he jibed:

'You can't blame her for getting the wrong impression when you drooled on about her making a wonderful mother-in-law. I expect you found it easy to get a dress out of her after that!'

Kim felt so humiliated she couldn't speak. She was sickeningly aware that he knew she had thought he was about to ask her to marry him. The mood he was in should have warned her that nothing was further from his mind. She was amazed at her own stupidity, but even more by Garrick's cruelty.

Through having to wait for the dress, which, in the end, he stubbornly insisted on doing, they were late in leaving and consequently late in arriving home. At Coolarie it didn't help that they had to wait for someone to collect them from the airstrip.

'Someone's head it going to roll over this!' Garrick fumed.

'It's my fault,' Kim whispered unhappily.

'I'll deal with you later,' he returned curtly.

Kim considered bleakly that his silence, as they had flown home, had been punishment enough. She didn't believe he had been sulking—he was too superior for that! He had just thought of other things and shut her out.

The truck, which finally arrived to pick them up, braked too abruptly. From the swirling dust a lanky station hand appeared.

'I'm sorry, boss,' he exclaimed, 'I didn't know I was to pick you up until a few minutes ago.'

'Why the hell not?' Garrick snapped. 'Where's Joe?'

'Joe?' the man fidgeted uncomfortably, glancing quickly at Kim.

'That's what I said,' Garrick's voice tightened with impatience. 'Where is he?'

'He's gone away.'

'Gone away—where?' Garrick demanded sharply.

'On holiday, boss. Him and his missus.'

'On holiday?' This time it was Kim who spoke, as she gazed at the young man incredulously. 'You must be mistaken. They might have gone somewhere for the day, but if they'd been going on holiday they would have mentioned it to me.'

'I think they decided in a hurry, miss,' the man fiddled with the brim of his hat. 'I believe you're to stay with Brian until they get back.'

Kim had never seen Garrick so angry. Not even in the little seaport of Derby when they'd had to wait for her dress, had he been so incensed. After one glance, which had noted in him a sort of controlled savagery, she didn't look again until they reached the homestead.

'Would you mind dropping me off?' she asked him as they approached Joe's house.

Garrick roared past it, pulling up outside the office. Here he dismissed the station hand and ordered Kim inside. 'I want a word with you.'

There was no escape. She felt like running, but there was no where to run to. No place here where Garrick couldn't find her. For the first time in weeks she regretted Coolarie's isolation. Garrick went into the office and she followed reluctantly. Telling her curtly to take a seat, he closed the door.

There was a note on the desk. Ripping it open, he read it before throwing it over to her. 'Read that,' he said roughly.

The print on Joe's letter danced before Kim's eyes as she sensed Garrick's disgust. Joe must have been in a hurry, because his note was extremely brief. He merely said he was taking Rose on a second honeymoon. That she hadn't been well lately and she needed a break. They would be back in a couple of weeks. Meanwhile, Kim could stay with Brian and look after him.

'Did you know anything about this? Anything at all?' Garrick rapped, as she lifted dazed eyes to his face.

'Well——' she hesitated, remembering how Aunt Rose complained frequently of headaches and feeling sick, 'I——'

'So you had an idea,' Garrick cut in furiously, 'and you never said anything?'

'Garrick——' she began, then stopped. What business was it of his, anyway? Surely Joe was entitled to a holiday before the Wet set in, when, from what she had heard, they might be marooned here for weeks. As usual, though, she found it easier to defy Garrick in her mind then with actual words. With his harsh gaze on her she could only swallow and reply weakly, 'I seem to remember Aunt Rose saying she could do with a break and I think I said I'd be all right on my own, if she and Joe wanted to take one. That's all . . .'

'I see.' Garrick stared at her frostily. 'You really believe you could live with Brian for two weeks?'

The way he put it there was no mistaking the innuendo! 'You've a horrible mind!' she cried. 'Brian's my cousin!'

'He—is—not!'

Garrick spaced his words, as he was inclined to do when he wished to emphasise a point. With her he seemed to do it deliberately, as if he sometimes considered her to be a creature of low intelligence. Kim felt tired and fed-up. She was ready to admit there was a lot about Joe's family she didn't understand, but surely that wasn't her fault?

'Whatever do you mean?' she muttered.

'Perhaps before you encouraged Joe and Rose to go off, you should have asked them to explain,' Garrick said tersely.

Had she encouraged them? Kim's eyes clouded with

bewilderment. She supposed she might have done, simply by not raising any objection. 'I didn't know there was anything to explain,' she replied faintly. 'How can Brian not be my cousin?'

'Because he happens to be the son of Joe's brother. His real parents died when he was a baby and Joe and Rose adopted him. They couldn't have any children of their own.'

Kim went pale with surprise. It didn't seem possible! She stared at Garrick blankly. 'I had no idea.'

'Don't your parents know?'

'No,' she shook her head in confusion, 'I'm sure they don't. They would have said. After all, adoption is no disgrace. Is Brian aware that he's actually Joe's nephew?'

'Yes,' Garrick was so emphatic she couldn't doubt him, 'they told him years ago. Naturally it made no difference to Rose and Joe—they worship him, but my father advised it.'

'And Brian? Did it make any difference to him?'

'I'm not sure.' Garrick's mouth thinned. 'The way he sometimes treats them makes me wonder. About Joe I don't give a damn, but I don't like seeing Rose hurt. She's too good for either of them.'

It was a lot to digest all at once. Kim saw Garrick looking at her shrewdly and felt strangely resentful. 'I'm sorry you had to be the one to tell me this,' she whispered, 'but you don't have to feel responsible for what happens to me. Surely I can still stay with Brian? I still regard him as my cousin.'

Garrick's dark, handsome features hardened as he came round the desk to jerk her to her feet. 'You little fool!' he forced her to meet his glittering eyes so she couldn't pretend not to hear what he was saying. 'You know you can't stay with him. I've seen the way he looks at you—he certainly doesn't regard you as his cousin. You'll stay at the house with Abby and me.'

Warm relief washed over Kim, but she had to ignore it. Garrick couldn't really want her, and why should he have to suffer her presence for a fortnight? And from her own point of view, to be in such close proximity to him for that length of time might be a bad thing. Already she was over-fond of him. Wouldn't two weeks of his company push her over the brink? Whatever happened, could anything be worse than being irrevocably in love with a man who didn't love her? Despairingly she wished Joe and Rose had never left, or that they had waited and taken her with them.

Hardening herself against the sensuous impact of Garrick's hands on her shoulders, his warm, clean breath on her face, she said jerkily, 'I wouldn't dream of troubling either you or Abby to that extent. I can always stay with one of the men's wives. Mrs Green wouldn't mind having me, I'm sure. Especially now that Jon's gone.'

Garrick put back his strong head and laughed. 'Don't you think it might upset Mr Green, though? Once he begins comparing you with his cosy, middle-aged wife you might regret going anywhere near them.'

Kim hated Garrick's mockery. She'd be willing to bet this was the first time he'd ever given Sid Green his full title. 'I should be flattered that you seem to imagine every man on the station is after me,' she snapped. 'I'd like to know what you think it is that attracts them!'

If she had meant to disconcert him, she was the one who was disconcerted when he answered, 'Do you really want me to spell it out? There's your youth, for a start. Sweet and twenty—and your figure. And your lips, which always seem waiting to be kissed. Like this.' Grimly he bent his head and his mouth moved briefly, passionately over hers while his arms slid around her tightly to crush her fleetingly against his whip-hard body. Anger appeared to be the driving force behind the hurt he inflicted, but his assault was shortlived as he almost forcibly thrust her from him.

'Now will you stop playing the little innocent and

make up your mind? Do I throw you to the wolves or
do you come quietly with me?'

'You act as if you're the biggest wolf of the lot!'
Carefully Kim touched her bruised mouth, amazed at
the damage he could inflict in just a few seconds.

'Miss Grantley, I asked for an answer, not a character reading,' he snapped.

Suddenly she surrendered. Garrick was so big she
couldn't fight him. When she tried she always lost—
hadn't she bruises to prove it? 'I'll stay with you,' she
gulped, 'if you really want me.'

'I do,' something flashed in his eyes she couldn't
quite make out, 'but the price is rather more than I
care to pay. Come on,' he added curtly, as her eyes
widened, 'I haven't time to stand here all day. We'll go
and collect your things.'

'I can manage to do that myself.' She dragged her
mind from his peculiar observation. 'With Uncle Joe
gone you must have plenty to do.'

'Nothing I can't manage,' he said dryly, 'but don't
be surprised if I call on your services. My mother
swears you're a miracle in the office.'

Kim smiled but made no comment, as she didn't for
a minute take him seriously. He probably wouldn't let
her within a mile of the office. At Joe's house he
insisted that she packed everything she was likely to
need for at least two weeks. He puzzled her by stating
firmly that she wasn't to return for any reason whatsoever until Joe came back.

'I should come and tidy up occasionally,' she protested as Garrick thrust her suitcase in the same truck
which had brought them from the airstrip. 'Brian won't
bother, and what will Aunt Rose think if she comes
home to a dirty house?'

'I'll get one of the women to see to it,' Garrick
assured her shortly, 'but don't worry, Brian will
probably manage better than you think.'

Abby was delighted to hear she was going to stay.
'It gets lonely here with Mrs Lang away and Garrick

out all day,' she beamed. 'We can keep each other company.'

'Just as long as you remember the evenings are mine,' Garrick teased. 'I promised, didn't I, to help you improve your swimming and tennis?'

The prospect of spending the next two weeks or so in the same house as Garrick suddenly didn't seem as frightening any more, and she smiled at him tentatively as she followed him upstairs. He showed her to a pretty room opposite a bathroom. 'This is really Abby's job,' he grinned, 'but as I was coming up anyway, it will save her legs. She's always complaining about them.'

Kim loved her room, which looked out over the gardens and was much more comfortable than the one she had at Joe's. The thick carpet was nice and there was a large armchair to relax in when she wanted to be by herself. The wide bed had a lovely rosebud cover while the windows were hung by curtains of a matching chintz. I won't ever want to leave, she thought ruefully.

Her only worry was Brian. She didn't know if he would approve of her being here and she wasn't sure what she was going to say to him. It had stunned her to learn that he wasn't her cousin, and she wondered what her parents would say when she got home and told them. Of course, she would have to ask Aunt Rose's permission before she could do that, and perhaps she wouldn't want them to know.

Kim didn't see Brian, nor did he seek her out, so after a few days she began to forget about him—at least she stopped worrying about him. First thing in the morning she helped Abby, then after breakfast she often went with Garrick to the office. Surprisingly, he had asked her if she would like to give him a hand, and she had agreed willingly. She told him honestly that she wasn't a properly trained secretary and only acted as a part-time one for her father, but he didn't appear to mind. He gave her only simple things to do at first, such as typing out letters which only required brief replies and making cheques out for him to sign. It surprised Kim, the vast amount of money it took to run a station like Coolarie.

'It certainly does,' Garrick said wryly, when she remarked on this. 'More goes out than we seem to have coming in. It takes quite a lot of doing making a station pay in these parts. You need a lot of irrigation and fertiliser and good men, none of which comes cheap.'

Kim was so interested and full of vitality, it was inevitable that she progressed rapidly. Garrick was soon leaving her to deal with some correspondence on her own and getting her to update records on his pedigree stock. He always checked her work, of course, but so far he had had no complaints.

If her secretarial work improved, so did her tennis. After several admittedly gruelling lessons from Garrick she was able to play quite a decent game. On the first Sunday of her stay, when Garrick invited friends over, she knew she acquitted herself admirably. She was much more thrilled, though, by the friendly arm he flung round her shoulder and the warm kiss he planted on her cheek in full view of everyone. He seemed not to notice the gently raised eyebrows or curious glances.

It was only her swimming which remained at almost exactly the same standard. That was mainly because she tried to swim in the afternoons when Garrick wasn't there. Her memories of the pool in the river were still too fresh. She found she couldn't face being in the water with him again, so soon.

In the evenings, after dinner, they either played records or strolled in the gardens, if Garrick wasn't working. The harmony between them surprised Kim and she stopped trying to hide the delight she found in his company. Sometimes she would put a dreamy dance number on the stereo and ask him to dance with her. Once, she trembled to remember, he had pulled her much closer than was necessary and laid his cheek against hers. And in the garden, as her confidence grew, she often slipped her arm through his. The previous evening, when she had done so, he had paused to turn up her face and kiss her gently. It had been a tender kiss, nothing passionate about it, not even in the way he had held her, but somehow it had seemed to hold more promise than any of his other caresses.

The incident in the shower shook her, but that same night, when he apologised, everything appeared to go on more or less as before.

There wasn't a lot of time before dinner, which was why Kim decided to have a shower, rather than a bath. It had been a long day. Before breakfast she had helped Abby, as usual, then afterwards, Garrick. He didn't often ask her to work in the afternoons, but today he had. They had worked until after six, when he had laughed and said she could go home and beautify herself for the evening.

Kim didn't know what had made her say, 'Soon your mother will be home, Garrick, and Uncle Joe and Aunt Rose . . .'

As she broke off abruptly, he had glanced at her enquiringly. 'So?'

His coolness confused her and she had blurted the first thing to enter her head. 'I'll miss having dinner with you.'

Garrick's eyes had remained expressionless. 'I'm sure my mother won't mind you joining us occasionally.'

'No, of course not,' she had stammered, feeling horribly embarrassed.

Suddenly he had smiled. 'Don't worry, Kim, I know exactly what you mean.'

She had glowed at him then, feeling terribly happy that their intimate evenings were beginning to mean something to him. Impulsively she had rushed to where he still sat behind the desk and kissed his hard, rugged cheek. The feel of him had made her breath catch and she flushed wildly as he tensed.

But his voice, when he spoke, had been teasing. 'You'd better not do that too often, young woman, or I might start getting ideas!'

Trying to hide her immediate regret and confusion

over her spontaneous action, she had resorted to returning his banter. 'I wouldn't really mind if you did!'

'Well,' he had stared at her a little more severely,
'don't tempt me, unless you're serious.'

She hadn't been quite sure how to reply to that, and
thought a light shrug might be safest. She had always
sensed that it might be dangerous to try and play the
liberated sophisticate with Garrick. Outwardly he
appeared to be a hard, unemotional man, but under-
neath he probably had more than his share of libido.
Although she kept a cool smile pinned to her lips, Kim
had retreated, with more haste than dignity.

Relaxing in the shower as the water washed away
some of the tension caused by her own foolishness, she
tried to think of someone other than Garrick. Mrs
Lang was feeling much better after her treatment in
Perth. From Joe and Rose there had been no word,
but when she had mentioned to Garrick that she was
anxious about them he had told her not to be.

'They'll be home when they're ready,' he had said
enigmatically.

Drowsily her thoughts returned to Garrick and the
love she had for him. It had grown since she had come
to live here, but she no longer feared it. Most of the
time he was so pleasant to her she didn't regret falling
in love with him. It was only on very rare occasions
that something about him made her feel apprehensive.
She knew she would love to spend the rest of her life
with him, but until lately she hadn't allowed herself to
hope he felt the same way about her.

But because a man was attracted to a girl, it didn't
necessarily mean he would ask her to marry him. She'd
be a fool to believe Garrick Lang would ever ask her to
be his wife, Kim told herself severely. And yet . . .

Wistfully she rinsed the last of the soap from her
long, slender legs and turned off the water. Water was in
short supply until the Wet came and she tried to use only
a trickle. Sweeping her damp hair from her eyes, she
reached for the shower door, and found it had stuck.

CHAPTER SEVEN

'Oh, no!' Kim exclaimed aloud, gazing at the glass partition in dismay. Shower doors never stuck, it couldn't be much that was stopping it from opening. Impatiently she tried again, but it refused to budge. Using pressure, she ran her fingers down the glass and, when it still wouldn't move, applied some soap against the joint, which achieved precisely nothing.

For the next few minutes she thumped and shook it, cajoled it without getting anywhere. She even tried climbing out, but the tiled shower walls were high and there was nowhere to get a grip with her feet. She actually scraped one until it bled on one of the aluminium uprights, which forced her to relinquish this method of escape.

Finally exhausted, she slumped helplessly to the floor, rubbing her sore foot. People were trapped in lifts, but whoever heard of it happening to someone in a shower? No one would believe her. She would have to get help, but where? No one, apart from guests, ever came here. And she had locked the bathroom, door which might make it almost impossible for anyone to hear her.

Nevertheless, she shouted until she was hoarse and each time she paused to regain her breath she tried the door, without success. When someone did come at last, it was Garrick.

Somehow she managed to make him understand her predicament, but she winced as she heard him put his shoulder to the outer door and crash through it. While the lock hadn't been a strong one, she didn't like to think she had been the cause of any damage.

'I'm in here!' she choked, hearing him swearing

softly as he approached. 'The door seems to be stuck, I can't get out.'

'Have you tried?' his voice came caustically.

'Of course I've tried!' she gasped. She could see the big shape of him through the glass but was so agitated she forgot he could see her. 'What do you think I've been doing all the time? Please, can't you get me out of here?'

'Keep calm,' she heard him mutter dryly—too dryly. 'I haven't heard of this happening before, but I suppose there's a first time for everything?'

'Please hurry!' she pleaded, a sob in her voice.

'If I can't open the door I can always fetch a ladder and you can climb over the top?'

'Very funny!' she croaked, not mentioning that this was exactly what she had been trying to do.

Suddenly, to her utter amazement, the glass partition between them glided smoothly back, revealing Garrick with his hand on it. He had obviously had no difficulty whatsoever in opening it!

'What on earth did you do?' she gulped, forgetting, in her surprise, that she was naked.

He didn't move. He stood there, all six foot three of him, a short robe tied around his middle, ending well above his knees. He had his own bathroom and must have been under the shower himself, because his hair was still wet. His eyes glinted as they roamed over her, the grey darkening with suppressed anger.

'What did I do?' he rasped, without removing his glance from her. 'I merely placed my hand on it and pulled.'

'But I've been doing that for ages!' Kim exclaimed hysterically. 'It was stuck tight! I tried and tried!'

At that moment she realised with startled horror that she had nothing on. The dizziness which had briefly blanked out her senses as Garrick had opened the shower door receded, and she felt like hitting him for the mockery she clearly read in his face. 'Oh, go away!' she screamed, huddling away from him as she attempted to hide herself. Shock and sheer exhaustion made her want to weep. 'Where's my towel?' she whispered, when he didn't move.

'Why defeat the purpose of the exercise?' he drawled, 'I prefer you as you are.'

Whatever did he mean?

'Come here.' He lifted his arms, his eyes hooded but his voice soft.

'A towel!' she snapped.

Suddenly he reached for one, but draped it around her so that her arms were completely trapped. 'You're ingenious, I give you full marks for trying,' he jeered, taking hold of her so she couldn't move and lifting her bodily out of the shower cubicle. Dropping her down at his feet, he tightened his arms as he lowered his head and began kissing her ruthlessly.

He held her so close she couldn't find her breath, and his sensuous kisses made her head spin. When the pressure of his mouth eventually eased she found only enough breath to ask unsteadily, 'Why do you think I'm ingenious?'

'Forget it.' His mouth explored her cheek, and as he found her lips again a flame shot through her. She trembled as he went on making silent love to her. She could feel her heart pounding and her blood heating as his expert caresses fanned the flame already inside her. She tried to think clearly, but was being swallowed up in a dark void. 'Abby?' she moaned distractedly. 'Dinner . . .'

Garrick merely laughed, easily controlling her feeble struggles. 'I might make a meal of you,' he said thickly. Almost savagely he thrust her back against the wall of the shower, his thighs moving against her, his flat, muscular stomach pressed tightly over her own. His mouth came down and crushed her lips, burning against them until he received the response he sought. Then, when she was clinging to him blindly, he thrust the towel that covered her aside and his hands and mouth began bruising the softness of her full breasts.

She felt the pain of it and the excitement as the tension between them craved satisfaction, turning the mockery in his eyes to unconcealed desire.

Her bones were melting as he made love to her, and she abandoned herself to his arms. When he drew slightly back she was breathing thickly and didn't know where she found the strength to whisper, 'Don't!'

Cynically he smiled, his mouth twisting as his eyes smouldered slowly over her, no mercy in their darkening depth. 'Come now, sweetheart,' he drawled mockingly, 'don't tell me, after all your careful plans, you're getting cold feet? If you are it's the only thing about you that's cold.'

Her senses swimming, Kim tried to reason things out. In Garrick's voice and eyes there was something she failed to understand. He might be a sensuous man, but she felt instinctively that he wouldn't normally act like this with a house guest. Something appeared to be goading him, driving him, but even as she searched frantically for the answer, he gave her no chance to discover what it was. Just as she was about to ask him, he began a further assault on her trembling body as his mouth closed over hers fiercely in a kiss that went on and on.

Then Abby was calling up the stairs from the hall, as she banged the old-fashioned, seldom used metal gong. 'Does anyone want any dinner tonight?'

Slowly Garrick took his lips away from Kim's, staring for a long moment at her hot, flushed face and muttering something under his breath. Controlling his mounting passion more easily than she did, he steadied her coolly as she swayed. When he replied to Abby his voice was deeper than usual, but carried smoothly. 'Begin serving it up, Abby. I'll be down in a minute.'

Kim was grateful that Abby dined with them that evening and the conversation was subsequently general. She found it difficult to even look at Garrick, and felt almost relieved when he said one of his neighbours was coming next day to look at some stock and would probably be staying. This neighbour, Neal Witton, had been in touch just before he left the office and this was the first chance he had had to mention it.

'It doesn't matter,' Abby smiled, 'Kim and I will cope. Mr Witton isn't difficult to entertain.'

'I'm sure nothing would be beyond Kim,' Garrick smiled obliquely.

Across the table Kim's eyes met his and his glance wandered cynically over her. She was wearing a pretty dress with her hair floating loose as she had had no time to arrange it in any other style, but she knew Garrick was seeing her as she had been in the shower. The pink in her cheeks deepened and she hastily lowered her eyes to her plate.

The mystery of the shower door continued to plague her. Garrick didn't believe it had been stuck. He believed she had only pretended it had been in order to entice him into the bathroom. Kim's cheeks kept going hot when she remembered how he had kissed her. Even under the waterfall his mouth hadn't been so hurtful. She was miserably aware of his thinly veiled contempt and that nothing might ever be the same again.

After dinner, when he went to his study, it was almost an hour before she felt brave enough to go and knock on the door. As if he realised who was there, his voice, when he commanded her to enter, was very short indeed.

Knowing he was angry with her didn't do anything for Kim's equilibrium, but as she stepped towards him her blue eyes pleaded with him. 'Garrick, I realise I've made you angry, but the shower door really did stick.'

'We can forget about that.' he didn't lay down his pen as he looked coolly at her, which seemed to suggest he wanted rid of her as quickly as possible.

This started up in Kim a kind of panic. 'You can,' she burst out, 'because it didn't happen to you. It wasn't a terrible experience, although it was a bit alarming, but it *is* terrible that you doubt my word!'

'Yet not all that important, surely?'

'It is to me!' She didn't care if she was saying too much. It was the truth anyway, and she wanted things right between them.

Garrick sighed, though his mouth was no less grim. 'Do you always have to be so dramatic, Kim? If it will make you any happier, I apologise for saying things you obviously had no wish to hear. Now, if you don't mind, I'm busy.'

'The standard excuse,' she muttered, turning bleakly away.

'Kim!' He was at the door before her, taking hold of her and shaking her gently. 'If I was angry in the bathroom it was because I didn't think there was any need for you to tempt me so far. How would you have felt about me in future if I'd followed my inclinations and told Abby to forget about dinner and made love to you in your room instead?'

'You—you wanted to?' Her eyes widened in incredulous confusion while every pulse in her slender body raced.

He laughed harshly, as if at himself. 'What do you think?'

'Why didn't you?' she asked, without stopping to wonder what he would make of such a question.

'Is that an invitation?'

She flinched at the derision in his voice. 'No,' her face flushed, 'I—I just wondered.'

'Well, I suggest you stop wondering and asking such forward questions, Miss Grantley.' Opening the door, he pushed her almost roughly through it. 'One of these days you might find yourself with a permanent resident in your room, but I think you need a little more time.'

Abby fortunately didn't appear to notice the broken lock on the bathroom door. Garrick fixed it next morning so that it was almost impossible to tell it had been damaged. Kim admired the neat job he made, but knew it would always remind her of what had happened inside.

When Neal Witton arrived, she spent the day hoping he might get stuck in the shower, for that might be the only way to convince Garrick that his suspicions about her were unfounded. But although Neal took two showers, one in the evening and another the following morning when he got up, nothing in the nature of what Kim had hoped for occurred. While he was in the bathroom, she haunted the vicinity, waiting for the cry for help which never came. Eventually she was forced to the humiliating conclusion that it had been something she had done—or hadn't done—that had made the shower door stick, and it was a waste of time trying to prove her own innocence as it might never happen again.

Neal Witton was, as Abby had hinted, a very pleasant man. He was tall and dark, like Garrick, and about the same age. His parents were American and both his father and grandfather, he said, had put a lot of money into sheep and cattle properties in Australia. Both he and his sister Beth had been born here.

He was a lively talker and made Kim laugh a lot. And she felt oddly grateful that he seemed to take some of the strain from the atmosphere. After dinner, although they just sat around, she was surprised to find how quickly the evening went. Neal wasn't married and he stared a lot at Kim, who, perhaps in defiance of Garrick's continuing aloofness, wore a little more make-up than usual and a slightly more daring dress.

Before he left, Neal asked them all to a barbecue and dance his parents were giving. 'We're hoping to beat the Wet,' he said when Garrick glanced at him enquiringly. 'Beth being away visiting held things up.'

'When did she get back?' Abby asked.

'Only the day before yesterday.' Neal glanced quickly at Garrick, who said nothing, then turned to Kim. 'She's looking forward to meeting you. It's not often we see someone from England. I'll be able to tell her how lovely you are.'

'You'd better not!' Abby exclaimed, then looked

quite flustered as if she wished she hadn't spoken, while Garrick simply looked grim.

What it was all about, Kim had no idea, and she didn't allow herself to get curious. There seemed enough mystery at Coolarie without looking for any more.

The following day, however, she did ask Garrick if they would be going to the barbecue.

'Someone will take you,' he replied shortly, 'don't worry.'

'I wasn't,' she swallowed nervously, still feeling the rift between them. 'I—er—don't you attend such functions?'

'Sure I do,' he smiled. He was sitting at his desk in the office and crossed his hands behind the back of his head as he leaned back.

Kim wished he wouldn't. It was a habit of his when he wanted to eye her speculatively and it outlined his big body in a tantalising way. She had never really noticed a man's body so much before. Lately she'd been scarcely able to look at Garrick without shivering. Like a lovesick adolescent, she thought uneasily, wishing it hadn't been something more than that!

'Then why pretend you aren't going to this one?' She was so alarmed by the strength of her feelings that she found herself snapping.

'I'm not pretending anything,' his voice was maddeningly reasonable, 'I'm merely saying I don't go to them all.' Unperturbed by her crossness as she glared at him, he added smoothly, 'I imagine the whole station will be going to Wampoola, so you wouldn't lack company, but if you were to ask me nicely I might just take you myself.'

It was amazing how a few words could lift the spirits! Kim felt suddenly wildly happy, although she tried not to let it show too much. 'Why can't people hold parties in the Wet?' she asked after a moment.

'We do,' he shrugged, 'but it's not so easy to get about. And they have to be indoors.'

'It can't rain all the time, surely?'

'No, but for three months, sometimes longer, the rivers are flooded and the roads often impassable. And the storms can be quite violent, as you'll discover for yourself before you go home.'

Kim drew a sharp breath, going pale, not because of the impending storms but at the thought of going home. Bitterly she acknowledged that perhaps these little reminders that her time here was limited were good for her. Certainly Garrick appeared to enjoy dishing them out!

As the happiness she had felt a few minutes ago rapidly evaporated, she murmured rather flatly, 'I wonder when Uncle Joe and Aunt Rose will be home? They've been gone almost two weeks.'

When Garrick merely shook his head, she frowned. 'They haven't even sent a card, at least not to me. I don't suppose you know where they are?'

'No,' he replied curtly, 'I do not.' His face altering subtly at the mention of Joe's name, he began leafing through a sheaf of papers. 'We'd better get on,' he said coolly, 'I want to get finished here so I can go and see some land we've been improving on the other side of the property. The men have run into a few problems.'

From then on Garrick was pleasant to her, but strangely distant. After dinner, most evenings, he disappeared into his study, and Kim never found the courage to seek him out there again. Apart from a few hours in the office she saw little of him, yet she wasn't unhappy. She felt amazingly content just being near him, and knowing how emotions were apt to get out of control when they got too close, she persuaded herself that he was leaving her alone because of that. He must respect her if he refused to risk things getting out of hand again, and she wondered tremulously, not for the first time, if he might possibly have marriage in mind.

When Joe and Rose did return home she felt ashamed that she wasn't altogether pleased to see them.

She and Abby were busy in the kitchen after lunch when Rose startled them both by walking in.

'Oh, my!' Abby sat down with a gasp and a thump, 'what a fright you gave me, Rose! I couldn't have been more startled if you'd dropped from the skies!'

'There was no one at the house or I shouldn't be here,' Rose explained, after she'd said hello and apologised. 'We've had a lovely holiday, but Joe hasn't felt well or we might have stayed longer. We went to the coast, and it's done me the world of good, which is why I can't understand about Joe.'

'Perhaps he was just fretting to be home?' Abby smiled.

Rose frowned but didn't pursue the subject. 'Where is everybody?' she asked Kim. 'The house seemed deserted.'

'I don't know where Brian is.' Kim found her tongue at last and gazed at her aunt anxiously. 'Garrick thought I should come here after you'd gone, and I'm afraid I haven't seen anything of Brian.'

'I think he's been working away,' Abby said briefly.

Kim was silent, feeling oddly guilty that she hadn't even known that much.

'Where's Joe now?' asked Abby, after a quick glance at Kim's puzzled face.

'Can't you guess?' Rose sighed. 'He's gone to the office—I suppose to see if it's still there!'

'Garrick won't be there,' said Abby, 'but I'm sure Joe will find everything in order. Kim's been helping, so nothing's got behind.'

'He'll be pleased about that, but you know what he is,' Rose laughed lightly. 'I thought I'd managed to talk him into buying a lovely little house on the coast, but he decided at the last minute that Garrick couldn't do without him.'

Neither Kim nor Abby made any comment on this, and a few minutes later Rose said she must go back and asked Kim to go with her. 'It will take us all afternoon to get the place aired,' she said, a hint of reproach in her voice. 'I don't think there's been a window open since I left, and the rooms all smell musty.'

Kim followed, after Abby assured her she could manage the rest of the luncheon dishes herself. She didn't tell her aunt that Garrick had forbidden her to go to the house while she and Joe were away, because she wasn't sure if Rose would believe her. Garrick had also said he would get one of the women to look in, but if Brian hadn't been there he had probably thought that wouldn't be necessary.

'Have you heard from your parents lately?' Rose asked while they worked.

'Two letters.' Kim stretched to remove some dust from under a bed. 'They're fine.'

'Good,' said Rose briskly, then her brightness disappeared as she returned to the topic which always absorbed her most. 'I do hope Brian is all right, as well. I did think you would be looking after him.'

'I'm sorry.' Kim glanced at Rose uncomfortably, wondering what more she could say. She had decided not to mention that she knew Brian wasn't really her cousin. If she did, and Rose hadn't wanted her to know, she might only be hurt.

'I think you'd better go and see where Joe is,' Rose said, when everything had been dusted and polished to her satisfaction. 'I still feel worried about him, Kim. While you're away I'll make a pot of tea. See if you can persuade him to come back with you and have some.'

Aware that her aunt was anxious, Kim went immediately. She thought longingly of a shower and a change of dress, but her aunt's peace of mind was surely more important. It was hot—it had been hot all day; sometimes she had felt she was living in an oven. Of course, as she had to keep reminding herself, it was almost December, almost the start of the Australian summer. Having Christmas in the middle of summer must take a bit of getting used to.

Kim sighed ruefully. It seemed a long time since breakfast and the day wasn't over yet. She had her belongings still to collect from Garrick's house, and then Aunt Rose would expect her to help with dinner.

Heat hazed the distant mountains and the sun hung in a cobalt blue sky like a ball of fire. A slight wind stirred the dust as it lay awaiting the rains which must surely come to water the dry, parched land. It was a wild, primitive country and the ground was hard and red. Kim found it difficult to imagine floods sweeping down the river gorges and everything soaked to saturation point.

Garrick had gone out after lunch. He had taken the helicopter; she wondered what he was doing. Now that Joe was home again he wouldn't need her help in the office, and she realised she would miss the hours she had spent there with him. Unable to imagine how she might help him in any other way, she found herself growing quite despondent.

She was so busy thinking about this that she got quite a fright, on entering the office, to find Joe slumped over his desk. Shock halted her footsteps abruptly as she was sure he had collapsed.

'Uncle Joe!' she gasped.

As if her voice startled him, he straightened at once. His face was the colour of putty, but he seemed as alert as ever, and Kim's heart slowed down with relief, although she still felt shaken.

He stared at her, then, without preamble, asked loudly, 'Well, has Garrick proposed yet? You English girls, I'm told, are fast workers. Have you managed to bring him up to scratch?'

'What are you saying?' she whispered, her eyes widening with horror and contempt.

Impatiently Joe snapped, 'I'm asking if Garrick's asked you to marry him. Has our little plan worked?'

Whose plan? 'No!' Kim almost screamed back, and was going to add that she didn't know what he was talking about, when someone behind her cut in sharply, 'Nor am I likely to ask her to marry me, Joe. I'm sorry if that's what you've been hoping for.'

With a sharp cry Kim turned to find herself staring straight at Garrick. His powerful, rangy body filled the doorway. He had obviously been working, as sweat glistened on his face and bare, brown arms. He appeared strangely relaxed, but the eyes watching her were hard and dark.

'Garrick!' she breathed, crushed by a sense of impending disaster as she shrank from the icy contempt in his face. Suddenly she felt terribly cold. 'Garrick,' she whispered again, becoming apprehensively aware of what he quite clearly thought he had overheard. Yet, when she wanted to plead, to ask him to listen to her, her voice seemed to fail her.

As Joe's disgusted groan filled the air, Garrick gazed at her derisively. 'Give up, Kim!' he advised tersely. 'You don't have to pretend any more. I know why Joe brought you here, why you were so willing to come. It was a good try,' he glanced at Joe, 'but it won't work.'

As Joe shrugged almost carelessly, Kim went even paler and asked desperately, 'Will someone please explain what's been going on? What is it that I'm supposed to have done?'

Garrick's mouth curled. 'Are you trying to convince me you don't know why Joe sent for you?'

'I'm not trying to convince you of anything!' she exclaimed. 'I came for a holiday, that's all I know, because of Aunt Rose.'

'You didn't wonder why Joe should bother, after all this time? Why he should even insist on paying your fare?'

'No!' she cried, wishing he would stop speaking to her so harshly.

'I suggest, then,' he replied flatly, 'that you knew soon after you arrived here. And I might have fallen into the trap if Joe hadn't overplayed his hand.' He stared at her for another moment before turning grimly to Joe. 'When you asked me to meet your niece in Perth, Joe, you said you hadn't a photograph to help me identify her. But I happened to have seen a snapshot of Kim in the same desk as you're sitting at now. You must have mistakenly left it there, but I recognised her immediately. It was chiefly because of that as soon as I saw her my suspicions were aroused. I realised you were up to your old tricks again—but matchmaking ones this time.'

Kim was bewildered as well as angry. 'I remember wondering about the photograph when you mentioned it at the airport,' she admitted. 'I was sure Mummy had sent one, but I thought it must have gone astray, or perhaps someone had lost it. But you're crazy,' she rushed on, 'if you think I came to Coolarie expecting to marry you!'

Garrick eyed her steadily, his expression of contemptuous indifference hurting her almost more than his anger had done. 'It's Joe who's crazy, I think. I usually make a point of ignoring his little schemes. It's not so difficult and I've had years of practice. This is the first time I've been even remotely curious to see how far he would go—maybe because you were involved.'

'But I haven't been involved! I never was!' Kim protested wildly, seeing herself tried and condemned without being allowed even a few words in her own defence.

'Don't lie to me!' Garrick snapped suddenly, before she could draw another breath. 'One of the first evenings you were here, after I'd taken you home, I returned to ask if you'd do something for me—I can't remember what, but I incidentally overheard a conversation, or the end of one, between you and Joe which was fairly incriminating. And if I'd had any doubts, what I heard today would have swept them away.'

Kim licked dry lips, trying desperately to recall exactly what had been said on the night Garrick referred to, but failed completely. Garrick had kissed her, but he had left as soon as Joe and Rose had come in. Rose had gone to make coffee and Joe had begun talking about something, then the porch door had banged, startling them. But what exactly had been said she couldn't remember!

'Why should Joe want me to marry you?' she asked at last, as her mind remained stubbornly blank.

'Haven't you asked him?' Garrick taunted, glancing derisively at Joe, who sat shrunken and grey at the desk. 'Hasn't he mentioned that he doesn't want anyone here who might be determined to get rid of him?'

'Irene would!' Joe muttered defiantly.

Kim stared at her uncle. What was he saying? He didn't attempt to deny one word Garrick said. Nor did Garrick refute Joe's last statement.

Garrick appeared to lose interest. 'I'm afraid your holiday has proved a waste of time, Joe. You've been extremely foolish and I'll admit, in some respects, I have been too. I deliberately pretended to be interested in Kim to see how far she was prepared to go. You mustn't blame her that your plan didn't succeed—she gave me every encouragement.'

Kim went white as she met his cold, blank gaze, her own eyes tortured as she suddenly realised what he was saying. Impulsively she exclaimed, 'You can't believe I was acting a part? That everything that happened between us . . .'

'Nothing happened,' he sliced in curtly.

'I know.' The deep breath she took didn't stop her voice from trembling, but it did help her to go on. Her cheeks flushing scarlet, she muttered, 'I didn't mean in the physical sense.'

'Perhaps not,' he agreed sarcastically, 'but that wasn't your fault either.'

Kim caught her lip so sharply she felt a trickle of blood. 'I don't know how you can stand there and think such things, when you must know they're not true!'

Garrick merely looked bored. 'I think it's time you stopped playing the dewy-eyed innocent with me, Kim. At least Joe is to some degree honest regarding his intrigues. Once he's found out he never tries to pretend he's the injured party.'

Angrily incredulous, Kim gasped, 'You really are convinced that I knowingly helped him this time! If what you're accusing us of happens to be true, which I very much doubt.' Anxiously she gazed at Joe, willing him to back her up instead of sitting there, just staring through the window, looking the picture of guilt and wholly defeated.

Garrick watched them both for a moment, then sighed tensely. 'I have no wish to make an issue of this, Miss Grantley. Joe provides enough melodrama without anyone adding to it. I suggest now that you come with me and collect your things. I have a sudden urge,' he added grimly, 'to see you out of my house.

'Out of my life too!' he snapped, as with a last urgent glance at Joe, Kim was forced to follow him from the office.

Joe obviously wouldn't hear this last sentence, but that was little comfort to Kim. 'I'll leave right away!' she cried. 'I don't want to stay another day!'

'Good.' Garrick didn't appear to mind that she had to run to keep up with his long strides. 'If you need any transport I'll give it top priority.'

Kim would have left that minute if she'd been able to. She wished there had been some means by which she could have simply disappeared! She wasn't sure if she could endure much more of Garrick's unswerving contempt. Unhappily she wished things could have been different, but there was no magic wand she could wave to wipe out everything which had happened.

Nevertheless, despite her growing anger, she made one more attempt. 'You've got it all wrong,' she began.

'Suppose you let me decide?' he interrupted harshly.

'I don't have to,' she panted. 'I'll be glad to leave, if only to get away from you, but that doesn't mean I'm guilty of the dreadful things you accuse me of. If I ever thought I was beginning to get—get fond of you, you've certainly cured me!'

'Let's not go into the improbable state of your emotions,' Garrick's voice chilled her to the bone. 'Few women manage to love anyone but themselves.'

'We aren't all the same.'

They had reached his house. Abby was nowhere to be seen, for which Kim was thankful. Garrick hustled her inside, his hand grasping her arm painfully when she hesitated. Coldly he ignored her last protest.

'Come on,' he snapped, 'I'm in a hurry if you aren't.'

'I can manage on my own,' she gasped. 'There's no need for you to come with me.'

'I intend seeing you personally off the premises,' he retorted icily.

In her room he stood over her, checking each drawer and cupboard as she emptied them.

'Don't worry,' she said bleakly, 'if I did happen to leave something I wouldn't come back for it.'

'Wouldn't you?' he sneered cynically.

'No, I would not!' Kim's voice wobbled, but he didn't seem to notice. 'Garrick,' she paused in her packing, her face white and strained, her mind worrying over what had happened, unable to leave it alone, 'why won't you believe I knew nothing of what Joe had planned, or what he was supposed to have planned? I find it hard to believe he left me here in order to tempt you to get seriously involved with me, but if he did I had no part in it.'

Suddenly Garrick's control appeared to snap. His hands reached out, taking hold of her swiftly as he exclaimed harshly, 'I want no more of this, Kim. Perhaps Joe hasn't told you everything, people often get so steeped in their own intrigues that they can't bear to reveal very much. It's a kind of self-protection. But, as I said before, I refuse to add to the drama by discussing it. It's sufficient that you were willing to go along with it.'

'You must have enjoyed yourself, encouraging me,'

she said almost fiercely. 'I suppose all that about owning so many stations and being wealthy was all part of the game? And you dare accuse me of being melo-dramatic!'

His lips curled thinly while his hands hurt her shoulders. 'If you hadn't acted so deliberately naïve, I might have resisted the temptation to exaggerate my financial status somewhat. Few girls seem able to resist the wealthy grazier image.'

'So you're really poor?' she said, trying to speak coolly.

He let go of her sharply. 'It seems a shame to disillusion you,' he drawled. 'Certainly my wife won't be getting mink and diamonds.'

Kim felt sickened when she realised that was what he thought she had been after. 'They wouldn't be much use to her here,' she choked. She paused, her eyes meeting his wildly, her breath a ragged sound. 'But from what I hear, Mrs Ross will be able to supply her own!'

CHAPTER EIGHT

IMMEDIATELY Kim spoke she regretted it. Brian hadn't asked her to keep the information to herself when he had told her about Irene's money, but he might have expected her to.

'So someone's been talking?' Garrick's grey eyes were frosty.

Kim shrugged and got on with her packing.

'Who?' He hurt her shoulders again as he swung her around to face him, but her wince didn't appear to bother him.

'I don't have to say.' She felt so tired and depressed, she didn't find it too difficult to continue defying him, but suddenly, to her horror, tears began trickling down her cheeks.

'Oh, for God's sake, don't give me the full treatment!' he jeered, pushing her away. 'It's not hard to guess where you got your information from. It's no secret, anyway, that Irene is a wealthy widow.'

Surreptitiously, Kim sniffed, wiping her eyes with the back of one of her hands. As her hands weren't exactly clean, after her afternoon's work, dark smudges were left on her face. Catching a glimpse of herself in the mirror, as she inadvertently turned her head, she was startled by the dishevelment of her reflection. Her long fair hair was loose and untidy about her tear-stained features, while her dress seemed to be clinging damply to every taut line of her body.

Suddenly she didn't care any more, and the hurt inside her enabled her to retort outrageously, 'Perhaps when you marry Mrs Ross she'll be prepared to be generous with her money!'

'Of course,' Garrick drawled, so softly that Kim

wasn't surprised to see his eyes darkening with anger. 'But I don't have to discuss my future, or the woman who might share it, with you.'

'I'm sorry,' Kim apologised humbly as his mouth tightened threateningly. She didn't think she had any need to apologise, but what did it matter? What did anything matter now that Garrick had more or less openly admitted he was going to marry Irene? Kim's heart, already aching dully, was assaulted by a fresh wave of pain.

He made her feel even worse when his eyes narrowed and he said abruptly, 'If you're quite finished, let's get out of here. I'll send someone over with your suitcases. And,' he added, as she nodded obediently, 'when my mother returns you are not—and I repeat, not—to oblige when she asks you to help her.'

'Don't worry,' Kim whispered, her face a shade whiter. 'As I intend leaving at once I don't suppose I'll see her again.'

'Now that's really good news,' he taunted. 'You did say you were leaving, but I wondered if you'd changed your mind.'

'You can't wait to see the last of me, can you?' she said hoarsely.

'I can't pretend I'll be sorry.' He gave a mirthless laugh. 'Can you blame me?'

'No.' She didn't feel like arguing.

'What will you tell Rose?' he asked suddenly, as she walked past him out of the bedroom which she had occupied so happily for over two weeks. She had been living in a fool's paradise!

'Rose?' Jerking her thoughts from her own stupidity, she stared at him almost blankly for a moment. 'Oh, I see. I—well, I suppose I'll just tell her I'm needed at home. I've already mentioned that I've had two letters. I'll just say I've been reading between the lines, or something like that, and believe they're missing me.'

'As ingenious as ever?' he mocked.

Kim's anger flared, finding its way briefly through

the pressing weight of her misery. 'What would you expect me to say? That I'd fallen in love with you and my heart was breaking?'

'Which wouldn't be true?'

Kim stumbled, falling to her knees, but while she felt humiliated by her sudden clumsiness she was also relieved that her fall had saved her from answering his question.

By the time Garrick dragged her impatiently to her feet, she had managed to find some kind of control. 'I've had a good holiday,' she told him hollowly. 'Plenty of girls only manage two weeks. I don't think Aunt Rose will mind all that much.'

'Good.' As though his mind was not wholly on what she was saying, he swept her out the front door. 'I may not see you again before you leave, so I'll say goodbye.'

'Goodbye,' Kim echoed dully, not trying to stop the tears from pouring down her cheeks again—tears from which he grimly averted his eyes. For a moment he appeared to hesitate, then without another word turned and went back in the house.

Kim ran all the way along the drive, careless of who might be watching or what anyone might think. She felt ashamed that she had allowed Garrick to see how unhappy she was. If he hadn't left her so quickly she might have told him she was unhappy because of leaving Coolarie, not him. Perhaps it was just as well he hadn't waited; at least she had been spared having to tell a lie.

Again, as she hurried, she tried to hide her heartache with anger. He hadn't even said thank you for all the hours she had worked in the office. If he had offered payment she would have felt insulted, but he might have spared her a few words of appreciation. That wouldn't have cost him anything!

As her tears threatened to turn to a wild deluge, she sought shelter under some trees, knowing she must have a few minutes to compose herself before facing

Rose. She wanted nothing more than to throw herself on the hard red ground and sob, but that was a release she must deny herself. She would have to learn not to weep if she was to face the future with any equanimity. There would be no Garrick, and the sooner she accepted that the better.

Burning with humiliation and pain, she leaned against a tree and stared out over the distant plains. How he must have laughed at her, despised her! All along he had believed she had come to Coolarie solely to marry him. That she hadn't shrunk from his kisses or his company must have helped to convince him of that. The incident in the shower had clearly confirmed his suspicions, while what Joe had said, as she'd entered the office an hour ago, must have quickly removed any last, lingering uncertainty.

But if it was true that Joe had hoped Garrick would ask her to marry him, what had he expected to gain from such an alliance? A permanent foothold on Coolarie, obviously, without having to worry any more about Irene Ross. Cynically Kim thought Joe might be worrying unnecessarily about Irene Ross. Not for a moment did she believe that Garrick would allow any woman, even his wife, to do anything at Collarie which he didn't agree with.

Well, from now on Joe would have to look for another solution to his problems. Tomorrow she would be gone. Things could only become worse if she lingered on. Bleakly, her decision to leave strengthening resolutely, Kim returned to Rose.

'Where've you been?' Rose asked sharply as Kim walked slowly into the kitchen. And before Kim could answer, 'When you didn't come back I went to see what was keeping you, but your uncle Joe said you'd left the office.'

'Where is he now?' Kim asked, wondering anxiously how much he had told Rose.

'Oh, still there,' Rose sounded worried. 'He wouldn't come home with me.'

When Rose said nothing more, Kim felt instinctively that Joe had told her nothing. 'I've been packing my things at Garrick's house,' she said suddenly. Nervously, as Rose glanced at her, she drew a deep breath. 'I don't quite know how to put this, Aunt Rose, but I'm afraid I'll be leaving Coolarie in the morning.'

'Leaving Coolarie?' Rose sounded completely bewildered and looked it. 'Why, whatever for?'

Kim searched desperately for a convincing excuse. 'I think I'm homesick. And, reading between the lines of Mummy's last letter, I can tell they're missing me. I think I'd better go.'

'But you've only been here a few weeks!'

'Which is longer than the normal holiday,' Kim replied, trying to keep her voice light.

Abruptly Rose sat down, as if she didn't know what to say. She stared anxiously at Kim, her work-worn hands knotted tightly in her lap. 'It's nothing I've done, or said, is it? Joe and I shouldn't have gone off and left you as we did. I didn't want to . . . Oh, well,' she flushed painfully, 'that doesn't really matter, but if it's anything I've done wrong and can put right . . .?'

'No!' Kim laid her hand on her aunt's arm affectionately, hating to cause her pain and hating Joe and Garrick more for being responsible for it. 'It has nothing to do with you, Aunt Rose.'

Rose went on as though Kim hadn't spoken. 'I haven't been very good company, dear, I'm afraid. I've grumbled too much about my headaches, but you see, I've never had a daughter to complain to. Joe and Brian are good, but they don't want to hear of my aches and pains. Having you here seemed to go to my head,' she smiled rather mirthlessly at her own unintentional pun, 'another woman in the house, I mean, to moan to occasionally.'

Kim gave Rose's arm a loving little shake, trying urgently to get through to her. 'You rarely if ever complain, Aunt Rose, and I've never minded helping or listening. I tell you what,' she smiled gently, 'when you get your dream house on the coast I'll come back again. I'll begin saving up right away!'

Joe was late in coming in and Rose asked if she would delay mentioning her departure until the morning. 'He might feel better after a good night's sleep,' she whispered to Kim as they drained the vegetables for dinner. 'He doesn't look well, and if we tell him now he might only blame himself and worry, and I'm frightened that that could make him really ill.'

So Rose must know something. Kim would have liked to have asked how much her aunt knew, and if she considered Joe's fears regarding Mrs Ross were well founded. Then she decided against it. No amount of talking could change anything now, and might only make matters worse.

Kim didn't sleep until after dawn and woke with a start to find Garrick shaking her.

'Garrick?' she exclaimed, utterly startled as she stared up at him as he loomed over her. Still thinking she must be dreaming, she did nothing immediately to cover herself up. It had been hot during the night and, in her restlessness, she appeared to have thrown off her sheets. Her brief nightdress seemed to be crumpled around her waist and only her pale gold hair covered her. Fortunately it hung in thick, silken strands over her shoulders, allowing only a little creamy skin to show through. The eyes she raised to the man beside her were swollen by recent tears, but were blue and sweet, very innocently appealing.

'Oh!' she choked, realisation suddenly dawning as Garrick's glance darkened and burned over her. A painful flush coloured her cheeks as she hastily grabbed a sheet, pulling it over her bare body. 'How dare you come into my room like this? I—I'm not ready yet,' she stammered, thinking he had come to take her to Derby himself. He must want to be very sure he was rid of her, and was giving her no chance to change her mind.

'I haven't come to help you quickly off the property,'

he snapped, 'although I'd like to. Joe's ill. Brian came for me, and the doctor's on his way. He should be here any minute, but Rose needs your help.'

'What's wrong with Uncle Joe?' Kim's own troubles paled into insignificance beside Rose's greater ones.

'I think he's had a heart attack,' Garrick answered grimly. 'I could be wrong, of course.'

'I'll get up at once,' Kim said jerkily, 'if you wouldn't mind leaving.'

He turned immediately, but paused by the door to look back. For a moment the world seemed to contain only the two of them as Kim enquiringly met his eyes. 'Be as quick as you can,' he said harshly, and she thought, unnecessarily.

As the door closed behind him, she scrambled into the first clothes she came across, her fingers fumbling as her anxiety for both Joe and Rose made them curiously unsteady. She had noticed Garrick's grim gaze on her suitcases, the light jacket and handbag flung on top of them and the room stripped of her personal belongings. He couldn't have mistaken that she was ready to leave and hoped he was satisfied.

In the hall she found Rose talking to Garrick. Garrick turned to her. 'The doctor's just gone in. Joe doesn't appear to know anything of your eminent departure?'

Kim glanced quickly at Rose, who said, before Kim could intervene, 'He wasn't well yesterday. I asked Kim not to mention that she was leaving for fear of making him worse. I thought it would be wiser to wait until this morning, and,' she confessed frankly, 'I hoped to persuade Kim to change her mind.'

In a way Kim was grateful that Rose hadn't allowed Garrick to believe she was responsible for Joe's collapse, but she doubted if it would improve his opinion of her. Anxiously she asked Rose, 'Can I do anything to help?'

'I'm not sure——' Rose began, when the doctor joined them, causing her voice to fade apprehensively.

'How is he?' she whispered, her face white.

The doctor's very calmness was reassuring. Kim saw how it helped her aunt. 'I think we'll have to take Joe in to hospital, Mrs Petre. I'm not altogether satisfied with my own diagnosis and there are no facilities here to run tests. He's quite willing to go, but before we leave he would like to see his niece.' He glanced at Kim enquiringly.

Garrick quickly introduced them. 'Is it absolutely necessary?'

Dr Hamilton frowned. 'He seems very anxious about something—and disturbed. Whatever it is, it isn't helping his condition. If there's any way you can set his mind at rest, Miss Grantley, I'd be grateful if you would do so—that is if it's at all possible.'

While Rose turned to her imploringly, Garrick took Kim's arm and almost propelled her to Joe's bedside. She hadn't more than a few seconds to wonder what he wanted to see her about. Perhaps he was going to ask her to forgive him for what he had done? She would have to, as he was so ill, but she still felt sore at heart. It wouldn't be easy to pretend, but she might be forced to, for Rose's sake.

Despite her lingering animosity, Kim felt an over-whelming surge of pity when she saw how ill Joe looked. His face was grey and lined with pain and it was obvious that he found it difficult to talk. Yet as soon as he saw her, his face seemed to light up. It was almost as if he had been afraid she wouldn't come.

'Kim?' he struggled for breath. 'I—I wanted to ask, while I'm away, will you continue helping in the office?'

Kim's half smothered gasp brought the doctor's eyes sharply to her. 'Is that what you've been doing?' he asked, his voice for her ears alone.

'Yes, but——' she faltered helplessly.

'Then tell him you will. Say yes,' he urged impatiently.

Kim felt frozen. Garrick still grasped her arm and

she felt his fingers tighten. Apprehensively she stared up at him. Despite the urgency in Dr Hamilton's voice she was unable to speak.

It was Garrick who answered for her. 'Naturally she will continue to help me in the office, Joe. Don't worry—we'll manage, won't we, Kim?'

'Yes, Joe,' she agreed weakly.

Joe didn't appear satisfied with her faint reply. Hoarsely he asked, 'Are you sure?'

'Of course!' Kim realised hollowly she had to convince him. 'I'll stay until you come back and are able to take over again. I give you my word.'

Joe tried to smile, but although he failed he did seem more relaxed. Garrick let go of Kim's arm and began conferring with the doctor on the best way of getting Joe out to the airstrip. Rose would go with him. She would stay near the hospital, if necessary. She didn't know how long she might be away.

'You will be here when I come back, though?' she entreated, as she kissed Kim before leaving.

'Yes,' Kim promised, feeling hopelessly trapped. She realised Garrick might blame her for the situation, but what else could she do?

She didn't go with them to the airstrip. Brian went and Garrick. She hoped neither of them would return until she'd had time to consider her next move. If there was a way out of the dilemma she was in, she needed time to think of it.

Eventually she thought she had the problem solved. When Garrick reappeared alone, she wondered if Brian had gone with the others to look after his mother. While Garrick had been away she'd been so busy thinking she'd forgotten about tidying up, and as he walked in, she saw him glancing distastefully at the general chaos which Joe and Rose had left behind them.

She met Garrick's grey eyes warily, not caring for the expression in them, but before she could speak he asked abruptly, 'Is there any coffee or tea?'

'I'll make some.' Used to obeying him, she moved automatically to the kitchen, more conscious of his footsteps behind her than of anything else. Perhaps tea was a good idea. She'd had nothing at all since getting up and she felt quite shaky.

While the kettle boiled she cleared some space on the table. 'Would you like something to eat as well?' she asked politely.

'No, tea will do,' he answered curtly, staring at her.

'Garrick?' Aware of his sharp scrutiny, she looked at him again. 'I don't intend staying, you know. It was just to keep Joe happy.'

'You promised,' he replied tightly.

'I realise I did.' she put out two cups and found a tin of biscuits. 'What else could I do?'

'So,' he drawled icily, his eyes like gimlets on her strained face, 'how do you propose escaping your obligations this time?'

'This time?' she stared at him angrily. 'What do you mean, this time?'

'You appeared to wriggle out of the first agreement you made with Joe over me,' he rejoined caustically—and, she considered, unreasonably, 'so let's hear how you intend getting out of this one.'

'I hate you!' she whispered fiercely, two hectic rings of colour on her cheeks.

'You probably do,' he agreed silkily, 'and perhaps it's just as well. I wouldn't want you concentrating on me, rather than the accounts.'

'You can't seriously mean that?' she exclaimed. 'I mean, about the accounts. Don't you understand? You don't have to take this thing seriously. As far as I can see they won't allow Joe out of hospital until he's quite well again. And by then he'll be strong enough to realise that he's been quite unfair in asking me to remain here and work in the office. He'll probably be glad I didn't.'

The cool gaze levelled on her. 'That's just where you're wrong, Miss Grantley. You may think you have it all worked out, but Joe's no fool—not altogether. He was quite aware that you might scarper as soon as he was out of sight. I gave him my word that you'd stay—which, I might add, appeared to satisfy him much more than yours did.'

Kim stared at him, her vision blurred. 'Then you won't let me go?'

'Not until Joe is back, either to take over again or retire.'

Because she grabbed the boiling kettle without paying proper attention to what she was doing, the steam scalded her wrist. As with a muffled cry of pain she dropped it, Garrick took her arm and thrust it under the cold tap.

Behind her she could feel the pressing length of his hard body and his breath on her cheek as he bent to adjust the flow of water. 'Why do you always do such stupid things?' he muttered grimly.

Kim stood trembling as his words seared over her and she sensed their double meaning. It seemed so long since she had been this near to him and she had thought she had built up a certain defence, but she was alarmed by the sudden urgency of reawakening desires. He was so close she could almost feel the movement of his lips against her face as he talked. His arms tightened and she was aware of the tenseness of his body, of new pressures rapidly building up in both of them.

But he made no attempt to achieve a greater intimacy. He remained as immovable as a rock, although she heard him draw a harsh breath, but if he had been fighting his own inclinations the silent battle was soon over. With a curt word to stay where she was, he left her to deal with the kettle himself.

'How long will it be, do you think, before Joe comes back?' Kim asked bleakly, as the cold water cooled her skin but not her emotions.

'Two, maybe three weeks.' Garrick placed the lid on the teapot indifferently. His voice was quiet, but he seemed angry about something.

'But what about you?' Kim swung round, water dripping. 'You can't convince me you won't mind having me around for that length of time——'

'Maybe I do mind,' he snapped, 'but what else can I do? I won't be the first man to be trapped by his own principles into helping the enemy.'

'Surely Joe's not that?'

'A matter of opinion. Perhaps not in all ways, but enough to prove a continual source of irritation.'

Kim sighed. 'And you're willing to let me add to it?'

'If you want to put it that way, but I don't have to share that view. I consider that once a man discovers a girl's little game, it renders her completely harmless. From now on I'll treat you as a stranger. As for the office, I've already proved I need help there. And while I could quite possibly find someone else, I'd have to get to know them, and they probably wouldn't be any better than you.'

'So you can quite easily forget who I am?'

'Quite easily,' he smiled mockingly into her unconsciously hurt blue eyes. 'I've had several hours to cool down. From now, as far as you're concerned, I won't lose any more sleep. I shall merely consider you as a part-time secretary.'

'Very well,' she replied tautly, realising how Joe's health—even his life—might depend on her. But her heart felt as if it was breaking. Garrick knew how to hurt her, she could tell by the glint in his eye, and once he had started turning the screw she feared he might have no intention of stopping. He might forget, but that didn't mean he had forgiven. 'I'll work for you,' she agreed, 'but only for the next two weeks, no longer.'

'We'll see,' he retorted coldly, slamming his cup down on the table. 'I'll expect you at the office in half an hour,' he added, as he walked out.

Brian arrived home at midday, just after Kim had completed a hectic session with Garrick. She had done her best, which apparently hadn't been good enough, and his temper and offensive remarks had been hard to bear.

'Miss Grantley,' he had snapped, when once she had dared to protest, 'before you were a guest who had offered to oblige, and I didn't pay you. Now you're working for me for a salary, and I expect you to earn it.'

'I never was a secretary,' she managed to point out, in an attempt to ward off the sarcastic references to her incompetence which she was sure was coming.

'I realise,' his voice was cutting, 'and you'll be paid accordingly, but what you lack in experience you will make up for with hard work!'

Kim had stared at him, utterly wounded by his callous tones, then she suddenly burst into tears. Wholly dismayed because she hadn't wanted him to see how much he could hurt her, she had rushed from the office, but before she could reach the door he caught her.

Spinning her round like a top, he had grated, 'Wipe your eyes! I want no more hysteria. I promised Joe you could work for me but I won't put up with your tears. If you're going to collapse each time I speak sharply, you won't last five minutes.'

'It was different when you were pretending to be falling in love with me, wasn't it?' she cried wildly, and unwisely. As this seemed to silence him and give her the advantage, she rushed recklessly on, 'I wasn't greatly impressed by your prowess as a would-be lover, but it was much to be preferred to this!'

His eyes had sparked blue lights. 'If I hadn't realised your little game in time, I assure you you would have had no such complaints.'

'That, and of course the fact that you're pratically engaged to Irene Ross!'

'You catch on fast!' he had sneered.

'Just as well!' she had flung back, relieved to find a kind of impotent rage drying her tears. 'And I'll tell you this,' she glared at him, her blue eyes sparkling defiance, 'you—you can keep your precious money. I wouldn't take a penny!'

'Perhaps you'd prefer to be paid in other ways?' he taunted, his voice icy with a fury to match and surpass her own.

'Like what?' she asked sharply.

'Like this,' he retorted insolently, lowering his mouth ruthlessly.

'No . . .!' Her tremulous protest was cut off by the brutal force of his lips on hers, and his arms went completely around her, bringing her roughly against his large frame.

Kim went rigid, determined to fight with every ounce of strength she had. She felt incensed that Garrick should choose to treat her this way. Feverishly she told herself that his behaviour was a total insult, a true reflection of his opinion of her. With angry determination she kept her mouth tightly shut and began struggling.

He hadn't allowed it. Eyes smouldering, he had lifted his mouth a fraction from her own. 'Stop fighting!' he said harshly.

'You'd like that,' she had gasped. 'You'd like me to cower like a frightened rabbit while you walked right over me.'

'Be quiet!' he had snapped.

When she had taken no notice and tried to kick him, with a furious exclamation he had jerked her head back with a handful of hair while simultaneously one of his hands pushed under her soft vest to close savagely around her waist.

His grip had tightened, his fingers digging into her soft flesh as he pulled her against the vibrant warmth of his body. For a long, earth-shaking moment he held her, letting her recognise the superiority of his masculine strength, until she collapsed weakly against him. Then, again, his mouth had descended inexorably and slowly, the pressure he exerted becoming pain. Her whole body had seemed racked with it, as his arms had threatened to break her in two. Yet she had wanted to stay in his arms for ever and had been unable to hide the passion which began to consume her.

When eventually Garrick had pushed her away, she had groped blindly for the nearest chair, while he had merely opened the door and walked out. Kim had stared after him in stunned silence and could have sworn he never once looked back. She must have sat there for quite some time before she had managed to force her unsteady legs to support her and follow.

Wearily she had dragged herself home, relieved that Garrick wouldn't be needing her any more that day, knowing it might take her all afternoon to pull herself completely together.

When Brian walked in demanding lunch, she was startled. 'I thought you'd gone with Uncle Joe and Aunt Rose?' she exclaimed.

'No, I'd too much to do here,' he replied.

'But how will your mother manage without you?' she frowned. 'I'm surprised Garrick let her go on her own.'

'She won't come to any harm,' Brian shrugged, 'but as a matter of fact I am going, after I've had something to eat.'

'Lunch?' She gazed at him blankly.

He laughed, although his eyes narrowed. 'You sound as though you'd never heard of such a thing!'

'Oh, I'm sorry.' Flushing, Kim jumped to her feet.

'Okay, don't panic,' he grinned. 'Cold meat and a salad will do, even a sandwich.'

'I hope you father will be all right?' she said a few minutes later, setting a huge plate of sandwiches before him along with a pot of coffee.

Brian shrugged and began eating with obvious relish. 'He has a way of coming out on top, has my old man,' he observed cynically. 'I shouldn't worry too much, if I were you.'

'When you see him,' she said heavily, 'you can tell him I've been in the office all morning. If you're allowed to see him and he asks, that is.'

'And you've had a rough time of it, from the looks of you.' His glance again took in her pale face and rumpled appearance. 'I won't tell Joe that,' he assured her quickly, 'but I shouldn't let Garrick push you around, if I were you.'

'It's only for a week or two,' she flushed.

'Think you'll come out of it alive?' he taunted.

'I hope to do more than just survive,' Kim said stiffly.

'Well, I've got news for you,' Brian said suddenly. 'Irene Ross is home, so the boss won't have so much time to concentrate on the mistakes of lesser mortals like us.'

After he had gone, Kim washed up, then indulged in a positive orgy of cleaning. What she and Rose had done the previous afternoon she did over again, and didn't stop until she could go on no longer. Even then she still felt too restless to sit down, and she decided to go out—perhaps riding somewhere.

As she was leaving, Abby called. It was after six and Kim was surprised to see her. 'We've just heard about Joe,' she told Kim. 'He's to have an operation for a gastric ulcer.'

'So it's not his heart?'

Abby paused to regain her breath. 'That's not so good, the doctor said, but apparently he reached hospital in time and is in no real danger.'

'Aunt Rose must be relieved in a way,' Kim said anxiously, 'but I don't suppose she'll feel a lot better until it's all over. It's a good job Brian will be there with her.'

'When he gets there,' Abby sniffed dryly. 'When I saw him after lunch he thought he might not go until tomorrow. Comforting the sick, or those looking after them, isn't exactly Brian's forte.'

'But he promised he was going!' Kim looked at Abby in dismay. 'What will Aunt Rose do without him?'

'Brian breaks his promises as easily as he makes

them,' Abby sighed, 'I don't think he means to be deceitful, it's just that he's very easily distracted. Garrick's trying to discover where he is now, but there's no guarantee that he'll succeed. He could still be on Coolarie, for all we know.'

'Which won't help Aunt Rose!'

Abby's eyes sharpened on Kim's pale face. 'I shouldn't worry too much, dear. Garrick has everything under control. He's in constant touch with the hospital and Rose. If there's any danger at all he'll go himself. Rose knows she can rely on him absolutely.'

Kim felt herself tremble. Everyone, even Joe, whom Garrick made no secret of despising, could rely on him. She was the only one he wouldn't hesitate to break if it were possible. Hadn't he demonstrated that very clearly this morning? She still felt lacerated by the harshness of the treatment he had meted out to her. His kisses had been the final insult and she hated to remember how she had, if only for a few minutes, responded to him.

Despondently she remarked to Abby, 'It looks as if Uncle Joe could be away a long time.'

'A week or two, anyway,' Abby agreed.

Glancing at her quickly, Kim asked, 'Did you know that I promised Joe I'd help in the office until he gets back?'

Abby shook her head but didn't appear at all surprised. 'Well, perhaps it's better than having nothing to do, don't you think? I know I like to be busy when I'm worried about something and there's nothing I can do about it. Rose will feel happier, too, knowing you're here, keeping an eye on things.' She paused uncertainly. 'I'd be happier if you'd still been up at the house, but Garrick said you'd removed your things in a hurry because you'd been thinking of leaving.'

Realising, from the way Abby spoke, that this was all Garrick had said and she was curious, Kim admitted warily, 'I was . . . I thought my parents might be missing me, but obviously I can't go now until Uncle Joe is better.'

'No, I see.' Abby's brow cleared. 'Then how about coming back again, until Joe and Rose return?'

'Did Garrick ask you to ask me?' Kim asked, scarcely able to believe he would, yet unable to stop herself from hoping. Perhaps he had relented?

'To be honest, he didn't,' Abby confessed. 'He wasn't in a very good mood, so I didn't suggest it, but I know he wouldn't mind.'

'I think I'd rather stay here.' Kim tried to speak casually, to keep any betraying bitterness from her voice. She even forced a light laugh. 'Remember the fuss Aunt Rose made yesterday about the place not being aired? I don't want to be guilty of the same crime twice!'

'You're sure?' Abby smiled, but doubtfully.

'Anyway,' Kim remarked, as Abby turned to go, 'Mrs Lang will be home soon, and Brian told me at lunch time that Mrs Ross is back, so it looks as if you'll soon have enough to do without having to look after me.'

CHAPTER NINE

AFTER Abby had gone, Kim went for a walk instead of riding. She wandered for almost two hours before returning to make herself a light meal and going to bed. It was only ten, but she couldn't think of anything else to do, and in bed, in sleep, she hoped to find even a brief respite from her unhappy thoughts.

Brian hadn't come home, but she decided to leave the door unlocked in case he did. If he wasn't with Aunt Rose he might still be on Coolarie, and if he woke her by banging on the door she might never get back to sleep again.

An hour later, however, she was still awake. Try as she might, she found it impossible to stop dwelling on Garrick and Irene Ross. Consequently her heart was heavy and aching, as was her head, and sleep continued to elude her. She was just about to go and find some aspirin when her bedroom door was suddenly thrown open.

Believing it must be Brian, Kim jerked upright with a smothered cry. Then, to her great surprise, she saw it wasn't him but Garrick— A rather frightening, furious-looking Garrick, who, for the second time that day, appeared to be ruthlessly invading her bedroom.

'Not again!' she exclaimed, her voice a mixture of fright and defiance which changed swiftly as she realised he might have brought bad news. 'Is something wrong?' she whispered anxiously, 'Is it Uncle Joe?'

His grey eyes slanted darkly over her tense form. 'No, nothing's happened to Joe. I'm looking for Brian.'

Kim's relief was immediately replaced by angry

indignation. 'In my room?'

He brushed aside her taut query as if it was of no consequence. 'The outside door wasn't locked and you were nowhere around. I had to make sure you weren't lost somewhere. I saw you earlier on, wandering quite some distance from the homestead.'

'You could have knocked,' she protested, 'instead of coming in here!'

'Sorry, lady,' his apology verged on insolence, 'I did knock, and receiving no answer I came to the brilliant conclusion that you were either still out or asleep. If you were asleep, well and good, but if a person is missing in these parts we feel honour bound to start looking. Either way, there was only one way of finding out. If you were asleep I wasn't going to wake you.'

Kim might have replied that the way her bedroom door was thrown open had been enough to wake the dead, but suddenly she felt too weary to argue.

'Brian isn't here,' she sighed. 'He told me he was going to join his mother, that's all I know. I haven't seen him since lunch.'

'So Abby said.' His eyes met hers coolly. 'I was just checking, as he isn't with Rose yet and I'd like a word with him. Would you mind if I waited for a while in the lounge? He could turn up any time.'

'If you like.' Kim knew instinctively that he would, whether she agreed or not. Sensing he was ready to counter any protest she might make, she saved her breath. After all, he was the boss!

'Would you like me to get dressed and make some coffee?' she asked, as he stared at her suspiciously.

'No,' he retorted grimly, as if that was the last thing he wanted. 'I can make it myself if necessary. Are you all right? Can I get you anything?'

If the last two sentences hadn't seemed to be dragged out of him, Kim might have replied differently. Clenching her hands tightly against the coldness of his tones, she shook her head. 'I don't want anything—I'm fine.'

'Goodnight, then,' he rejoined, with a last glance at her small, huddled figure. 'I'll see myself out later, if Brian doesn't arrive.'

With Garrick in the house, Kim hadn't expected to sleep, but, strangely enough, his presence made her feel secure. While she puzzled over this she dozed off and didn't wake up until the next morning. Once, during the night, she dreamt that someone was standing over her, staring down on her, but when she woke the dream was so hazy that that was all she could recall.

Remembering that Garrick had been here and why, she dressed hastily and ran to the lounge. He had obviously been gone a long time as the lounge was empty, and, although she searched the house, there was no sign anywhere of Brian.

She had been working in the office for more than an hour when Garrick came in. She had been beginning to think he wasn't coming, but her feeling of relief faded when he appeared. As his sharp gaze flicked over her his eyes seemed to smoulder, and she wished wearily that he would stop being so angry with her.

He didn't explain his lateness, which made her angry, too. Why should he consider himself a kind of god, who could do what he liked? He obviously didn't give a damn that she'd been sitting here half the morning, waiting for him.

Leaning against the edge of his desk, he continued to regard her narrowly. Then he announced abruptly that his mother was returning home the following day. Before Kim could make any comment, he went on, 'She's bringing four friends with her, who will probably be staying a few days, so would you please move to my house again, Miss Grantley, to help Abby? I'll reimburse you, of course.'

Kim stared at him, feeling helpless. She didn't want to do as he asked, but she couldn't find an excuse. The one she knew might convince him would only make him laugh. 'If you think it's necessary,' she agreed reluctantly.

'I wouldn't have asked, otherwise,' he assured her curtly. 'My mother appears to be much better, but I don't want her pitching in and having a relapse.'

It was the last thing Kim wanted, to have to live in the same house with him again, where his nearness would only torment her. There was a trapped look about her as she gave in. 'I'll come, but I don't want to be paid for anything.'

His mouth twisted. 'I thought you'd be glad of the extra money, if you're in a hurry to get home.'

'I am,' she retorted, 'but Uncle Joe gave me my ticket.'

Garrick's eyes went chill. 'You could always repay him, seeing how you failed to keep your part of the bargain.'

His taunts fractured her control, but she tried not to let him see how much he could hurt her. She had a fierce urge to slap his contemptuous face—she told herself he deserved it. She might have tried if he hadn't looked so tired. He was pale, his mouth tight. He looked as if he hadn't slept. Rather than allow pity or anger to overwhelm her, she pretended not to have heard what he said and asked tautly, 'Did you find Brian?'

'Yes,' Garrick replied grimly, 'I believe he's just arrived at the hospital, but God knows where he spent the night.'

At least he didn't appear to believe it had been with her! 'Will he stay with Aunt Rose, do you think?'

'He'd better!'

Kim wasn't sure who his voice was threatening. Her gaze jerked towards him, but not all the way. She felt his eyes fixed on hers intently, but refused to meet them. Could he possibly be hinting that that was up to her? Hearing him move, she glanced at him furtively as he straightened. Had any man the right to look so attractive? This morning he was wearing a thin, checked shirt that stretched across his broad shoulders, and his dark pants were moulded to muscular thighs. His dark hair was well brushed but inclined to be unruly. And while his chiselled features might be rugged, there was no denying the sheer strength of personality clearly marked on them. Painfully Kim swallowed, averting her betraying eyes.

'When I come to help Abby,' she told him, 'I would rather not be treated as a guest, like I was before.'

'How would you like to be considered?' He turned back to her again.

Such coolness when she was a quivering heap inside! 'Just as an ordinary working girl,' she managed.

His dark brows rose. 'Abby takes her meals with us, and she's a working girl.'

'She's practically one of the family!'

'As you tried to be once.'

Kim jumped up, but he was suddenly beside her, his hand on her shoulder, pushing her down. 'Stay put, Miss Grantley, and control that temper. I'm going—there's no need for you to.'

Her face scarlet, she glared at him. 'If it hadn't been that I promised Joe, I wouldn't stay anywhere near you!'

Garrick merely looked bored as he strode to the door. 'When you've finished here don't forget to move your things back to the house.'

He seemed to forget she was not a trained secretary with sufficient experience to work on her own. Fortunately his overseer came in, a man used to working with Joe, and together they accomplished quite a lot before midday.

Abby was busy when she arrived. Garrick must have mentioned that she was coming, as Abby seemed to be expecting her. She asked no questions, just glanced quickly at Kim.

Apparently Garrick wouldn't be in for lunch. Abby was having a light snack in the kitchen and invited Kim to join her. Kim thanked her, but explained that she had already had something.

'You're getting too thin,' Abby glanced over her sharply. 'I'll have to fatten you up.'

'I'm the skinny type,' Kim quipped, excusing herself quickly before Abby could comment on the paleness of her face, which she was obviously about to. 'I'll take my things upstairs and leave you to finish your lunch in peace.'

Garrick did turn up for dinner, but immediately afterwards he disappeared into his study. During the meal he talked lightly with Abby but only addressed Kim once—and that was merely to ask if she wouldn't mind passing the salt. Kim felt hot tears pricking the backs of her eyes as she was forced to endure his harsh indifference. Abby was curious, she could tell, as she kept glancing anxiously from Garrick to herself, but no one said anything to enlighten her. Kim found herself almost looking forward to the next day when the house would be full of guests and no one might notice how Garrick ignored her.

When Mrs Lang and her friends did arrive, however, Kim was dismayed to see Irene Ross with them. It seemed she had met Mrs Lang in Derby and been invited to join the party.

'I hope it won't be too much for you, Abby,' Kim overheard Mrs Lang saying. 'I was actually surprised when Garrick invited the Bronsons at such short notice, and especially as it's so near Christmas, but, as he says, his father and Arthur Bronson were very good friends and they haven't been here for a long time.'

'I'm sure we'll manage,' Abby replied cheerfully. 'After all, it's only for a few days, and Kim's here. She's going to help and she's very efficient, as well as being such a nice girl.'

Kim retreated to her room, rather than interrupt them in the kitchen, but later Mrs Lang sought her out to say she was sorry about Joe.

'Actually, I saw Rose last night,' she smiled gently. 'Garrick told me about Joe's operation and asked me to call at the hospital. Joe's recovering fast and is making definite plans for retiring. I do believe Rose is going to get her house on the coast at last! However, that can all be decided in a week or two, when they get home again.'

Kim would rather have had her meals in the kitchen, but Mrs Lang insisted she joined them in the dining-room. The Bronsons were a nice, elderly couple. Their son was pleasant, too, but Kim wasn't so sure about their daughter-in-law. She and Irene Ross were apparently good friends and talked continually about people and places Kim had never heard of.

That evening Garrick ignored her completely and the two younger women followed suit. Kim was glad she was kept busy helping Abby to carry in the various dishes for the different courses. When at last she managed to sit down, no one seemed to notice her growing progressively paler, or how little she ate.

After dinner Irene put some dance music on the stereo and Garrick danced with her. Arthur Bronson's son danced with his wife while the older people disappeared to play cards. After two dances the two couples on the floor changed partners, but eventually Garrick returned to Irene. He held her closely, as though he had scarcely been able to wait to get her in his arms again, and Irene looked more than content.

No one spoke to Kim who sat like a small, frozen statue. She wanted to get up and rush away from them all, but her legs somehow refused to move. Although pain lanced through her, she was unable to prevent herself from recalling how it had been during the first days of Mrs Lang's absence. While Garrick and she hadn't danced, they had listened to a lot of music and talked. She tried hard to forget the strange contentment she had found in their conversation. They had discovered they both liked more or less the same things, and how the same things amused them. It had startled her, sometimes, how their thoughts had moved in exactly the same direction. Even in their bodies there had been an almost frightening degree of co-ordination. Of course she had to remember that Garrick had been acting a part, encouraging her, she knew now, to make a fool of herself.

Swallowing nervously, she tried to prevent a hollow sickness from rising inside her. Mutely she raised anguished blue eyes, to find to her dismay that Garrick was staring at her past Irene's dark head. His eyes, arctic cold, were fixed on her, even as his hand caressed Irene's smooth back. More clearly than words his expression told her she was spoiling his enjoyment just by being there.

Kim's body convulsed, bringing her to her feet with more haste than dignity. She stood for a second, seeking to steady her shaking legs, and was just about to leave the lounge when Irene dragged Garrick to a halt beside her.

'Oh, Miss Grantley,' she exclaimed, 'I'd like you to turn down my bed. I noticed you hadn't done it earlier.'

A faint pink edged its way into Kim's colourless cheeks. Anger flared in her eyes, then subsided. What was the use of feeling like killing the other girl? What did it matter how Irene treated her? 'I'll do it right away, Mrs Ross,' she replied, without looking at Garrick.

'I'd like a flask of tea by my bed as well,' Irene ordered coldly. 'Since my husband died I don't sleep very well.' She smiled slowly and seductively at Garrick. 'I get lonely.'

'We must try to find a better cure than tea,' he murmured softly.

Kim knew if she didn't escape she might be ill. 'Yes, Mrs Ross,' she choked. 'Please excuse me . . .'

Later, after she had seen to Irene's requirements, Kim cried herself to sleep. She managed it with a blanket about her head, over her ears, so she wouldn't hear Garrick's long legs carrying him to Irene's room which was only two doors from hers, along the corridor. But no blanket or tears could eliminate from her tortured mind the imaginary picture of Irene clasped in Garrick's arms as he made love to her.

She was in the kitchen by six next morning, preparing early tea, when Garrick came in and told her that he wouldn't require her in the office today but hoped she hadn't forgotten the Witton barbecue that evening.

Abby was busy at the stove, with her back to them, but Kim wished she hadn't been there. She didn't want to go to the barbecue and she hoped Abby wouldn't interfere when she refused. 'I'm sorry,' she replied to Garrick, 'I'd rather stay at home.'

'Neal Witton is very keen to have you.' His taunting eyes gave an unmistakable double meaning to his words. 'I more or less promised he wouldn't be disappointed.'

'Of course she'll go, Garrick!' Abby turned to sweep Kim's further protests aside. 'I was just thinking yesterday that she needs cheering up. I heard her crying last night as I went to bed. It's either Rose or Joe, or she's homesick. Either way, we'll have to do something to snap her out of it. A barbecue and dance and a nice young man,' she smiled kindly, 'might just do the trick!'

Kim felt a red tide flooding right up to her neck and wished she could have sunk through the floor. How could Abby have told Garrick she had heard her crying? She couldn't bear to think he might guess it had been over him. The way he insulted her, she was determined she would never let him bother her again!

'I have been worried about Uncle Joe,' she declared, feeling she must give some definite reason for her tears, if only to take the cruelly complacent look off Garrick's face. 'I still am. I'm sure I shouldn't enjoy myself.'

'Nonsense!' Abby laughed, 'If I'd been younger I'd have gone myself. You go, dear.'

'That's settled, then.' Garrick removed his piercing gaze from Kim's face. 'We'll have an early dinner, Abby—just something light.'

They flew to the party. They could have gone by road, but as some of the way would have been little more than unsealed track, Irene protested that it would take them all night to get there, and she didn't fancy arriving covered with bulldust. For once Kim felt grateful to the other girl. It wasn't that she minded travelling by road, or a little discomfort, but she had no wish to be closeted for hours in a car with people who might choose to pretend she didn't exist.

The barbecue was well under way when they flew into the Witton homestead. Neal Witton was there to meet them and took possession of Kim immediately. With a wide grin on his pleasant face, he whisked her off after telling the others to enjoy themselves. Kim was happy to go with him, to lose herself in the revelry, away from Garrick's all-seeing eyes.

The band was good, so was the atmosphere. There were a lot of people of all ages, most of them, Kim saw, dressed informally, like herself. Abby had advised her to wear either slacks or an ankle-length skirt, so the insects, if there were any, wouldn't bother her. Kim had settled for a skirt and a casual but pretty top with a low, cool neckline, and although no one in Garrick's party had complimented her on her appearance Neal wasn't slow to make up for them.

'You look absolutely charming,' he said, his eyes going quietly over her. 'I could eat you.'

'I'd stick to whatever's cooking on your barbecue,' Kim laughed. 'It smells delicious!'

'So do you.' He breathed deeply of her delicate perfume. 'Don't try to put me off.'

When he asked her eagerly if she would like to dance, she nodded and did her best to pretend she was having a good time. It seemed inexplicable that she was unhappy with Garrick but even more so away from him. Making a determined effort, she fixed a smile on her lips, keeping it there until her face was aching.

Neal held her at a formal distance while his eyes clearly stated he would prefer to hold her much closer.

'I wanted to ask you out when I was visiting Coolarie,' he said, 'but I got the impression you were—well,' he stammered and flushed, 'that you were more interested in Garrick.'

'Garrick?' Kim tried to appear surprised, to reply lightly and with amusement. 'Oh, he's very nice in his way. Of course I like him.'

'But——?' Neal prompted, as her voice suddenly let her down and trembled helplessly.

'He doesn't like me,' she whispered. To her horror, her eyes filled with weary tears and she didn't avert them quickly enough.

'So I'm too late!' Neal muttered.

Kim couldn't decide that his heart was broken, but whether he was sincere or not, she felt it would be foolish to encourage him. 'I'm sorry.'

Wonderfully perceptive, he drew her comfortingly closer. As his arms tightened, he laughed gently and ruefully. 'Do you know, woman, I've been dreaming all day of holding you clasped to my manly breast, but I never dreamt it would be to console you over someone else!'

Kim laughed weakly, firmly controlling her desire to succumb to such tempting sympathy or to wallow in self-pity. Wryly she said, 'Well, as the man in question doesn't love me, I could use a few kind words, but I'm not sure they're good for me.'

'Is there another girl?' Neal frowned.

'I think,' Kim answered with painful frankness, 'it could be Mrs Ross.'

'You aren't serious?' Neal stared at her. 'Irene's been around for years!'

What did that tell her? Kim derived no comfort from the slightly incredulous doubt in Neal's eyes. 'Childhood friends frequently discover they actually love each other. They often marry and live happily ever after.' As Neal's brows rose even higher, she added frankly, 'He's never pretended to be serious about me, so I have only myself to blame for allowing my imagination to run away with me. Not that it really matters, because I'll be going home soon.'

'Home?' Neal looked quite dismayed.

'I'm afraid so.'

'Then, if there's nothing between you and Garrick,' Neal spoke loudly and urgently, 'you must let me see you again before you go.'

The music stopped and Kim was startled to find they were right beside Garrick. It saved her the immediate necessity of replying to Neal, but she was faintly apprehensive of the expression on Garrick's face. It could have nothing to do with her, though, as he hadn't spoken to her for hours. Another girl had joined the party and Kim wasn't surprised when Neal introduced her as his sister Beth. She was very like him.

After edging inconspicuously to one side, Kim became aware of Garrick staring speculatively from herself to Neal, and when he asked her abruptly to dance, she wasn't surprised at the lecture which followed.

'I don't mind you proclaiming to all and sundry that we aren't friends,' he snapped, 'but I won't have you encouraging Neal. Not seriously. He's had one or two unhappy affairs, he could do without another.'

'At least it proves he has a heart!' she snapped back.

'And I won't allow a mercenary little adventuress like you to take advantage of it!'

Suddenly the tears she had stemmed in Neal's arms overflowed. The cruel savagery of Garrick's words might have released them and they flowed down her cheeks in a humiliating torrent. 'My—my handkerchief!' she gasped, groping for it.

With a muttered explanation, Garrick swept her behind a thick clump of bushes. 'For God's sake,' he thrust a spotless white square at her, 'dry up! If you think a few tears are going to soften me up you're mistaken.'

'I don't!' she choked, then helplessly, 'Oh, Garrick, you can't hate me all that much! After all,' she whispered bitterly, 'I didn't succeed in marrying you. You haven't suffered. I'm the one who's doing that . . .'

As her voice faded to a stunned silence as she suddenly realised what she had revealed, he merely taunted her farther. 'You're wasting your breath—and if it's your conscience that's troubling you, don't let it. I've forgotten everything that happened, and I can find plenty other women only too willing to help me.'

'It's not my conscience.' Impulsively, again, she allowed his caustic tongue to wring from her a pathetic confession. 'I loved you.'

For a moment he tensed. In the moonlight his mouth went curiously white. His glance sharpened on her abundance of fair silky hair, the downward curve of her graceful head and neck. Then he stiffened. 'Sorry, lady,' he grated, 'I don't believe it. Unless,' he paused suavely, 'you would care to prove it to me?'

'Prove it to you?'

'Don't look so damned innocent,' he snapped. 'You know there's only one way.'

Kim heard her breath shudder in her throat as she stared at him. There was a hard, brilliant glow in his eyes as they flicked over her. She suspected he was deliberately baiting her, perhaps curious, because she had sunk so far in his estimation, to see how far she would go.

'As I don't love you now,' she replied, amazed to hear her voice so steady, 'I couldn't prove anything.'

'So your love was the kind which can be turned on and off like a tap,' he rapped scornfully. 'Well, that kind doesn't interest me. It's just as well I found out in time.'

When another sob shook her, he seemed to lose all patience. Grasping her arm with fingers that hurt, he almost dragged her away from the noise of the crowds and the fires. 'Let's take a walk until you manage to control yourself.'

'You can't have had supper yet!' Kim protested, after a few yards, when she felt able to speak.

'A walk will improve our appetites,' he jeered. 'At the moment I haven't any.'

'Won't Mrs Ross be missing you?'

'Perhaps,' his voice contained a hint of irony Kim missed, 'but any setback only makes her keener.'

'But if she's annoyed she'll take it out on me, not you!' Kim hadn't forgotten how he had stood by and listened while Irene ordered her around like a servant.

'You'll just have to be clever, then, won't you,' Garrick retorted unfeelingly, 'and keep out of her way.'

Full of hurt resentment, Kim retreated into silence. Yet she was shaking inwardly, and far from being able to pull herself together, as Garrick had advocated, she could, by the minute, feel herself growing worse. His nearness was affecting her too much for her ever to achieve even a moderate degree of calmness.

She had no idea where they were going, or in what direction. With daylight rapidly fading and on strange territory, her feet kept stumbling, her thin, strapped sandals giving little support. At times she was almost glad of Garrick's helping hand, although it continued to hurt her.

They had covered some distance before he paused. As she turned to glance at him in weary enquiry, he startled her by running the fingers of his free hand across her upturned face. 'Dry at last?' he exclaimed, derisively.

She flinched at his cold tones but managed to reply evenly, 'If you'd let go of my arm, I'd repair my make-up.'

Instead of doing as she asked, he jerked her harshly against him. 'You can repair it in a minute,' he promised mockingly, bending his head to kiss her.

He took Kim completely by surprise. She had been convinced he would never kiss her again. When he had danced with her, his sharp taunts had turned it to a kind of punishment. This, she soon discovered, was a form of punishment too, as his mouth was both persuasive and cruel. He seemed to be stamping a brand of hate on her yet was reluctant to let her go.

A faint breeze rose about them, coming from the lonely plateaux, emphasising their isolation. It was a mixture of the heat of the day and the cool of the night, so softly sensuous as to stir the senses. Kim trembled as she felt herself slowly coming back to life, as Garrick and the warm wind fanned fires she thought she had successfully dowsed to dead ashes. As the kiss went on and on, one of her hands crept up the side of his neck. Weakly she tried to stop it, but drawn by the stronger force of her emotions, it curled in his dark hair, as if trying to bring him even closer.

He let go of her so suddenly that she feared his abrupt rejection of her could only have been prompted by anger. She fully expected to be marched immediately back the way they had come. In fact, she was so dazed and shaken by his rough kisses that when they did begin walking she didn't realise they weren't going in the direction of the homestead at all, not until it was too late.

Garrick rushed her along, and blindly she allowed him to. The darkness and her tear-filled eyes defeated her. It was only as they began descending into a small gorge and she heard the sound of a trickling river that she stared around in mounting apprehension.

'Where are we?' she gasped.

'A nice spot,' she thought she heard him laugh mirthlessly. 'It's private.'

'What can we possibly want to be private for?' she asked, trying to speak calmly.

'I could be wondering how much you love me.'

Shrinking from the mocking coldness in his voice, she tried to pull free of him. 'I think I hate you!'

He merely laughed again. 'What does it matter? A little hate adds spice, but you'd have to convince me.'

As the incline unexpectedly grew steeper, Kim gave a frightened cry as her feet suddenly slid out from under her. When Garrick, cursing beneath his breath, grabbed hold of her. Kim's own arms involuntarily clutched him. When they fell he was holding her cradled against him, and while the breath had been briefly knocked out of her, his arms and the grass on the slope prevented any real damage.

'What—no fight?' he asked, as she lay for a moment completely still, staring at him, her eyes startled.

Finding her voice, she muttered bleakly, 'Why should I fight you? If I did, you're stronger than me, I couldn't hope to win.'

'I'm glad you realise,' he retorted grimly. 'It's time, I think, that someone taught you a lesson.'

Her protesting little cry was smothered against the merciless pressure of his mouth. All she could do was lie stiffly in his crushing embrace until he raised his head slightly.

'Garrick!' Taking advantage, she tore her lips from under his. 'Please be sensible!'

'I am being sensible,' he muttered curtly. 'I mean to rid myself, once and for all, of your traitorous, beguiling image!'

'How can you do it this way?' she moaned, feeling scorched by his harsh, burning gaze.

'Let me show you,' he grated, his mouth leaving hers to travel with passionate softness to her throat, following a sensuous, determined path to the warm, inviting curves of her breasts, making her tremble wildly as he added. 'After a man possesses a woman, it's almost guaranteed he'll lose interest.'

Alarm kept her rigid while she tried to control her rising panic long enough to think clearly. As they lay on the hard bank above the river, she could feel the strength of his iron muscles pressing into her and his mouth like fire, scorching her bare skin. It made her feel bitter as well as frightened that she was finding it increasingly difficult to hold herself aloof from him.

'If you don't let go of me I'll scream!' she threatened.

'No one would hear you,' he taunted, as if the very

thought of it amused him. 'If they did, I doubt if anyone would interfere. They'd only think it was a pair of lovers having a quarrel.'

Anger welled through her, lending a fierce strength to her hands as she began furiously to push him away. 'All right,' she choked, 'so you've had your little joke, but this has gone far enough. You'd better take me back at once!'

For an answer Garrick started to kiss her again, and much as she tried to go on fighting him it proved a fruitless exercise. Burning and searing, his mouth closed over her own, crushing its silken softness as he sought to subdue her to his will. Soon, as her body began melting helplessly under his, fear faded as other emotions swept over her, and the sudden tremor that shook his lean frame was matched by the ripple of growing excitement that shivered over her.

What was the use of fighting? she thought, her senses swimming. If Garrick wanted her, whatever his reason, why not? Wouldn't it be something to remember, all the long, lonely years without him? She would never want to belong to another man, so why deny herself this one glimpse of heaven?

Sensing her surrender, he wrenched at her blouse and a button flew as it opened to his impatient hands. 'Kim,' he groaned, the words jerked out of him against his will, like a man fighting a losing battle for control. 'Oh darling, Kim . . .'

Swiftly, his eyes devouring her, he pinned her slender body with sudden force. Her skin, smooth and supple, seemed to excite him and his increasingly urgent caresses sent waves of primitive longing to her sensitised nerve ends. Without knowing what she pleaded for, she heard herself begging him huskily to love her as his hands teased her taut breasts until she felt she was dissolving in incredible sensation.

She wasn't sure what was happening to her, and suddenly she didn't care any more. What did it matter what Garrick did to her as long as he satisfied this yearning inside her? An overwhelming desire to belong to him completely was eating her up, and as he continued kissing her, the hard pressure of his mouth induced a kind of blind delirium. Fiercely her arms tightened around his neck and she trembled, clinging to him submissively as she felt his passion mounting and he welded his dominant male body more closely to her own.

CHAPTER TEN

IT seemed a betrayal of the worst kind when he suddenly lifted himself away from her.

'Garrick?' She tried to hold him, to keep him beside her. 'What's wrong?'

'It's time we were getting back,' was all he replied, looking broodingly down on her.

Very carefully she sat up, unable immediately to throw off the floating sensation which had rendered her almost insensible in his arms. 'If—if you want me . . .?' she whispered, trying to see his face through the mist that seemed to be swirling around her.

For an instant she thought he was going to strike her and shuddered away from him, the fright she received bringing her sharply to her senses.

'You never give up, do you?' he said harshly. 'I don't think you would have enjoyed yourself much, though.'

As she stared at him mutely, he returned her stare, his glance grimly assessing the stark whiteness of her face, her haunted expression. 'You'd better get dressed,' he advised when she didn't move.

Suddenly realising the disarray of her clothing, Kim began feverishly to straighten it. She managed her skirt, but her blouse wasn't so easy. 'What will people think?' she muttered, her eyes wide with shame and despair. 'I don't suppose you have a pin or anything?'

'No.' His hand went out to grasp the button, which was hanging by a thread. 'Keep still a minute!' he commanded as she jerked away from him. 'I'm only trying to help.' Taking the collar of her blouse, he turned it back, pulling the long thread through until the button was fairly secure against the material again.

'It doesn't look too bad now,' he said. 'No one would notice.'

It was inevitable, of course, that some people did. Next morning Kim was still thinking, although she tried not to, of the reception they had received from Mrs Ross. Not that Kim felt she could altogether blame her for being cross when she and Garrick had been gone for almost an hour, with no one having the slightest idea where they were. When they had returned, with Kim's mouth bare of lipstick, betraying the fact that she had just been thoroughly kissed, Irene had looked incensed.

For Kim Irene's contempt might have been bearable if Garrick hadn't ignored her so completely afterwards. He had taken Irene away and spent the rest of the evening dancing with her and obviously doing everything he could to make up for his neglect. Bitterly Kim wondered what sort of story he had told her, to have mollified her so quickly. It was only towards the end of the evening that his reconciliatory attention had appeared to wane. Kim had noticed him at the bar, which had been rigged up for the barbecue. Irene had still been with him, but he had appeared to be drinking whisky as if it was water and staring grimly into the distance.

Neal had been polite to her but left her severely alone, while his sister Beth had only spared her a few coldly curious glances. Most of the time Kim had sat alone on a seat under some trees. Other men did ask her to dance, but she was so quiet she knew they had found her poor company. Once, seeking desperately to escape the sight of other people enjoying themselves, she had wandered off by herself among the trees surrounding the homestead. Here the solitude had worked like a balm on her aching heart, until she had had the frightening conviction that she was being followed.

All the way home, as she had expected, no one spoke to her, although Garrick had glanced at her with disturbing frequency. Possibly he was wondering, she'd decided bitterly, if she was going to tell Irene exactly what had happened when they had been alone together.

It had been daylight when they had reached Coolarie and Kim hoped she would never view another sunrise with such despair.

She saw little of Garrick as the day passed, and on the few occasions when their paths crossed he barely acknowledged her. He appeared to have given up all pretence of working in the office, and as there was little she could do there on her own, she concentrated on helping Abby. The news about Joe was still encouraging. Although his heart wasn't good he was recovering well. Hearing this, Kim felt forced to look more cheerful than she felt, as she no longer had this excuse to fall back on.

The Bronsons were to leave the next morning. They were already worried about the weather. 'Is Mrs Ross going too?' Kim asked Abby.

'I haven't heard anything,' Abby went on mixing biscuits, 'but if she was it's unlikely she'd be going with them. The Bronsons always like an early start, though, so we'll have to be up in good time to see to their breakfast.'

When Kim woke it was very early, scarcely daylight. She wasn't sure what had disturbed her, but she was right in thinking something had. From outside, from somewhere along the corridor came the sound of a minor commotion. Fearing something had happened to Mrs Lang, she slipped on her robe and peered out.

It wasn't Mrs Lang, it was young Mr Bronson. He was talking to Garrick and he sounded extremely annoyed.

'I'd have it seen to as soon as possible, if I were you. Anyone could be stuck in there for days. The first night I was here it happened. If Mira hadn't come along to see what was keeping me, I might have been there yet!'

Kim gave a gasp of surprise as she realised Charles Bronson must have been caught in the shower, exactly as she had been, but as the two men turned, as if sensing her presence, she stepped back in her room and closed the door. Now that Garrick might believe she had been telling the truth, it didn't seem to matter any more.

Garrick sent word for her to come to the study before breakfast. 'It seems I owe you an apology,' he said grimly, as she stared nervously at him.

For the second time that morning Kim gave a start of surprise. When she had been summoned so abruptly, she had expected to be accused of defaulting again, but she knew immediately what he meant. She hadn't thought he would admit she had been right about the shower, if only because of the other factors involved. However, it soon became apparent that a brief apology was all the concession he was making. In the silence which ensued she quickly realised this.

Looking away from him, she explained dully, 'You weren't to blame, I found it hard to believe myself. Did Mr Bronson have much difficulty getting out?'

'Not after I went to investigate the noise he was making,' Garrick said tightly. 'I'll have the whole unit replaced. The mechanism's obviously faulty, probably through being little used and very old.'

Kim gazed down at the floor, wishing her mind didn't feel so blank. Her head ached heavily and she suspected her face was colourless. 'Was that all?' she asked at last.

Perhaps such a lack of encouragement didn't help, but he made no effort to detain her. After allowing the taut silence to grow, he merely nodded. 'Yes, you may go now.'

While Kim was helping to serve breakfast, Arthur Bronson's wife said to her, 'Mrs Lang has been telling me that your father is an expert on antiques.'

'Yes,' Kim felt warmed by Mrs Bronson's kindly smile, 'he has a shop and is often on T.V.'

Mrs Bronson was impressed. 'He must make a lot of money.'

'I'm afraid he's too much of a dreamer,' Kim smiled. 'We're always quite poor.' Catching Garrick's eye, she flushed uncomfortably. Inadvertently she had given him another piece of information to support his fortune-hunting theories. At least, judging from the harsh expression on his face, it would seem so.

'My husband and I are hoping to visit England next year,' Mrs Bronson went on. 'If you would give us your address we might look you up. I love antiques and I know I should enjoy having a look round your father's shop. You'll be home then?'

'Yes,' Kim replied soberly. 'I expect I shall be going home any day now.'

After the Bronsons had gone, Garrick took Irene back to Derby. Before he left he spoke to Kim in the dining-room, where he found her clearing the table.

Watching her closely, he said. 'I won't be away long, but while I'm gone don't go riding on your own. The weather looks unsettled.'

'I've plenty to do here,' she tried to speak coolly, 'but if I did go out and get lost, why should you worry? I'm not your responsibility.'

His mouth tightened. 'Everyone is on Coolarie, as I've told you before, and I haven't time to waste looking for you.'

That hurt, though she had to pretend it didn't. She merely nodded and heard him mutter something under his breath as his arms went out to catch hold of her.

'Are you going to take me seriously?' he snapped, his face pale, his eyes glinting with anger as she gazed at him defiantly. 'Or do I have to use tougher methods to convince you?'

As Kim shrank from him, in heart-thudding alarm, his grip on her shoulders tightened and he began to shake her roughly. His head bent and just when she thought he was about to pull her closer, Irene called his name from the hall. With an impatient mutter, he released Kim and disappeared. As his footsteps receded, she sat down at the table and buried her hot face in her hands.

She didn't stir until Irene finally departed and the front door closed behind her. As she came from the dining-room, Mrs Lang was just about to go back to the lounge.

'Ah, Kim,' she said, 'Irene's just gone, what a pity you missed her. Garrick was in a hurry, though. He's going to call and see Joe while he's in town.'

Kim swallowed, trying not to feel bitter. She would like to have seen Joe herself, and Rose, but he obviously hadn't thought of inviting her. He must love Mrs Ross a lot. Perhaps while taking her home he intended proposing to her? Kim realised that if she had gone she would have been an unwelcome third.

'Abby is short of a few things,' she said suddenly. 'I think I'll go to Fitzroy Crossing and do some shopping for her.'

'The weather doesn't look too good,' Mrs Lang frowned. 'I don't want you taking foolish risks, dear. The rivers often rise very rapidly.'

'Who would miss me if I were washed away? Sometimes I wonder if life is worth living?' Kim spoke lightly, but was unable to conceal an underlying bitterness that made Mrs Lang glance at her sharply.

Abby, fortunately, didn't argue. Thinking a change, even a short one, might put some colour back in Kim's cheeks, she made a list of the things she required.

Abby seemed to forget that Kim had only been once to Fitzroy Crossing and that had been with Garrick. Recalling his remarks on the way she had handled the Range Rover, Kim decided to take a smaller truck, one which looked as if it had already suffered several knocks. If she dented it again, she hoped optimistically that it might never be noticed. She wasn't foolish enough to imagine she could just get in and drive away. One of the young men who worked for Garrick was around and she asked him several questions about the vehicle, until she was sure she could manage it.

'I wouldn't spend too much time in town, if I were you,' the boy grinned, glancing wryly at the sky. 'Sure looks as if something's brewing up there.'

Kim promised she wouldn't. The truck was full of petrol and to her delight responded beautifully. She had no trouble at all with it. Even on the worst part of the road she felt she was in control. At Fitzroy Crossing she swiftly completed her purchases, and, after buying some lemonade to quench a growing thirst, she decided to go straight home. It would be foolish to ignore all the warnings she had received and the sky was darker than she had ever seen it since coming here. She had no wish to tempt fate by lingering longer than was necessary.

Unfortunately she didn't get far before the weather broke in earnest. Never had she seen such rain! It made a downpour in England seem like a light shower. Incredibly soon the track was reduced to a quagmire, and with a sinking heart she remembered she had another river to cross.

A quiver of sheer fright travelled right through her when she eventually arrived at the river. Never would she have believed a few hours ago it had been a mere trickle. Now, she saw, it must be at least a hundred yards wide and running fast. It was full of debris, too. Some of the logs floating past looked quite huge!

Afterwards Kim realised she had been very foolish in attempting to cross it, but it seemed to her that once she was over she was practically home. The bed of the river must still be hard, the ground all round was like concrete. All she had to do was keep her head and put her foot down.

With thunder rolling all about her, interspersed by vivid flashes of lightning, there wasn't time to think, but amazingly she appeared to be going quite well until she was almost at the other side. Then it was that her two front wheels plunged heavily into a hole in the river bed and no matter what she did they refused to move. Anxiously she tried reversing, deciding she must choose another path. She had a faint suspicion that somewhere, impossible though it seemed, she had gone badly off course.

Carefully changing gear, she tried a little acceleration, but nothing happened. The truck again refused to go either backwards or forwards. At last, forced to give up, she tried to assess the situation calmly. Although her eyes were unable to penetrate far through the mist of driving rain, she could see enough to realise the river was getting rapidly deeper. If she sat here much longer the truck might soon be covered, and she might never get out.

'But it's Garrick's truck!' she heard herself whispering aloud. If it was lost would he ever forgive her? It might be shabby, but it certainly wasn't old.

Then suddenly it dawned on her that if she didn't abandon it, and very quickly, she might never live to know whether he was angry or not. Yet the only alternative open to her was even less inviting. If she tried walking through the river, she could be swept away and never found again.

Opening her door, she thought wryly that a quick death must be preferable to dying by inches, and although the river swirled darkly and fast it couldn't be as treacherous as it looked. Taking a deep breath, she lowered herself apprehensively into it. To her great relief it wasn't too deep, no higher than her waist, and, with a regretful glance at the stationary vehicle beside her she began wading ashore.

She was doing quite well until her feet slipped and while she was briefly submerged one of the heavy logs she had noticed, caught her a glancing blow on the head. Though fortunately it didn't knock her out, for a few moments Kim saw stars before she managed to pull herself together sufficiently to make the effort to heave herself from the water.

Here, when her head cleared a little more, she crawled to a safer distance away from it. Unhappily she took stock of her present position. While she might have escaped the river, she was still about ten miles from Coolarie. She could walk, but she might easily get lost as a lot of the track would undoubtedly disappear as the deluge continued. The storm appeared to be increasing in ferocity, and while that couldn't affect her already wet clothing, the blow she had received from the log was making her quite dizzy. If she tried to walk home she might never make it. Eventually she came to the reluctant conclusion that her only hope lay in staying where she was. She was on the right road—even if it scarcely existed any more—and, in time, someone might find her.

Retreating still farther from the encroaching tide, she found the shelter of some trees. From childhood she had been told never go near trees when lightning was about, but this afternoon she felt it might endanger her more to stay out in the open. Her head was aching, but it didn't seem to be bleeding. There was only a large bump on her brow, and she wondered how it could make her feel so terribly ill.

As the afternoon wore on into evening, she slept intermittently. Once when she woke she wondered if she was developing a fever as she found herself hot and sweating, while the wind seemed cold. She thought of Garrick and the way he had been shaking her when Irene had called for him, but each time she tried to reason it out, a kind of haziness attacked her and she would lose track of what she was thinking about. Occasionally she was sure she heard voices, only to discover it was the rain and wind in the branches and leaves above her.

But the next time she woke it wasn't these things she heard, or her imagination playing tricks on her. Someone was actually there, although she couldn't immediately take in what was happening. Faintly through the rain, when she opened her eyes, she could see men and vehicles. Somewhere she could hear Garrick shouting. He seemed to be issuing sharp instructions, his voice sounding odd, almost savage.

Helplessly she groaned, knowing she had been right in thinking he would be furious.

She tried calling that she was all right, to let them know where she was, but no one appeared to hear her. She had no idea how long she had been there, but she was dismayed to find she could barely stand, let alone walk. When she forced herself to try she stumbled so badly she fell on her knees more than once in her efforts to reach them. The men were only a mere fifty yards away, but they might well have been as many miles.

Drawing nearer at last, she heard Garrick exchanging curt words with one of his aborigine stockmen. 'If you're sure the truck's there, I'm going to swim across.'

'It's there, boss, that's for sure,' the man replied, 'but no one could be alive.'

'Be quiet!' Garrick's voice cut like a whiplash. 'Get me a rope. If the truck's there at all, I'm going to get her out.'

'Garrick!' Kim was almost upon them and he turned as if shot, his lightning glance piercing the growing darkness to discover her swaying figure. As he stood staring, obviously stunned, she spoke again, her voice trembling in hoarse terror. 'Please—don't go in the river. I'll buy you another truck!'

'You little fool!' Suddenly he appeared to pull himself together, a livid expression replacing the gaunt whiteness of his face. 'What the hell do you mean by playing a trick like that?'

What did he mean? She put a hand out to him, seeking unconsciously for someone to steady herself against, then as suddenly she dropped it. It was clear he had no wish to help her. 'I didn't do anything intentionally,' she whispered.

He was near now, grasping her arms, not bothering to hide his mounting anger. 'Do you realise some of us could have gone in there and drowned?'

'You—you didn't have to,' she gulped, her eyes

stretched over her face, huge and strained with fright and delayed shock. Her head, which had ached all day, felt as if it was splitting, and Garrick refused to listen.

'Of all the stupid, brainless things to do!' he snarled. 'No one with the least bit of sense would have got themselves into such a situation! Would you mind explaining how you managed it?'

'I'm sorry.' She shrank from him apprehensively, never having seen his face so hard and contemptuous before. His eyes held an unholy gleam of fury and his jaw was so tight it was streaked with white lines. His hair was wet, plastered around his strongly shaped head, while the rain ran in rivulets down his broad, bare chest. Behind him on the ground lay what Kim took to be his shirt, which he must have discarded as he'd prepared to rescue the truck. That must still be worrying him, of course.

'I'm sorry,' she repeated dully, finding it increasingly difficult to focus. 'I'll repay any damage, I promise, as soon as the river goes down, if you tell me how much.'

'The river might not be down for months.'

'I—I'll get Daddy to buy you a new truck.'

'How?' Garrick taunted, looking ready to hit her. Then, as she swayed drunkenly, one of the men with Garrick muttered, 'The little lady's out on her feet, boss, and standing here ain't doing her any good.'

'You're quite right, Jeff,' Garrick agreed curtly, some of the blaze dying from his eyes. But that was all Kim heard as everything began fading away from her and she slid in an unconscious heap at his feet. She was vaguely aware of a pair of urgent arms lifting her, but that was all.

When she came around she knew at once that something was different. No longer was she under some trees by the river—the bed she lay on now was much softer. The rain was still coming down, she could hear it soaking the ground, and the heat hadn't gone. She felt she was burning and tried to thrust the sheets that were covering her aside. It was difficult to know what she was doing as she somehow couldn't find the strength to open her eyes. Her head didn't ache so much. She recalled it aching terribly.

Then she remembered the river. All through the night she had struggled with it, but it had held her firmly, refusing to let go. She presumed she had drowned and was now somewhere else.

'Kim?' a voice reached her, masculine and strong but very anxious. 'You're quite safe, sweetheart. Open your eyes and look at me. See for yourself!'

Had she been delirious—babbling? Making a great effort to do as she was told, she was startled to find Garrick beside her. She was in her own bedroom, at Coolarie, in her own bed, and he was sitting on the edge of it, bending over her, his eyes full of remorse and something else she tried hard to see. Uncertainly her glance flickered to the window. It was still dark. 'Have we just got here?' she whispered.

'No,' he replied grimly, his intent gaze darkening as he searched her pale, bruised face. 'It's been over forty-eight hours, but you've been unconscious most of the time.'

'I'm sorry . . .' she began.

Swooping, he silenced her with a gentle kiss. 'I don't want to hear you saying that again,' he muttered fiercely. 'I'm the one who should be apologising.'

'What for?' she asked, in some bewilderment.

'For the things I said when I found you.' His voice throbbed with emotion. 'I should have been shot, but I was half off my head with anxiety. You'll never know how desperate I felt when I thought you were in the river. I don't think I'll ever be as near going insane again. When I turned and found you standing behind me something seemed to snap, and instead of taking you in my arms and telling you how worried I'd been, I found myself shouting at you.'

Unable to take in the implications of what he was saying immediately, Kim whispered huskily, 'I shouldn't have gone to Fitzroy Crossing. I only went because I was so miserable. I thought you'd come home engaged to Mrs Ross. Oh——' her eyes filling with weak tears, she broke off with a dismayed little gasp, 'perhaps you are? Are you going to marry her?'

'Oh, God!' he exclaimed harshly, 'I never had any intention of marrying her. She was just part of my defence against a slip of a girl from the U.K. You might have been, but she was never under any illusion as to how I felt about her. We've known each other too long for that.'

'Then why did you take her to Derby?' she faltered.

'To get rid of her,' he confessed dryly, 'and I had to see Joe.'

'Had to?' Kim asked in bewilderment as something in his voice suggested that had been imperative.

'Yes——' Garrick hesitated then continued more firmly, 'Kim, I love you, I want you to be my wife, but because I've a lot of explaining to do, I wasn't going to ask you until tomorrow. I've been in constant touch with Douglas Hamilton—the weather's been too bad for him to get here, and he advised against anything that might remotely disturb you until then.'

Kim gazed up at him, her suddenly luminous eyes giving him his answer while her breath did strange things in her throat. Garrick was asking her to marry him! Never for a moment had she allowed herself to think seriously that he ever would. But mightn't he only be saying that to comfort her? Tomorrow he might have changed his mind. She remembered his confusing behaviour in the past and the soft glow in her eyes faded painfully.

As he saw her uncertainty, a dark shadow crossed his eyes. 'I can understand the way you feel,' he said thickly, 'but you don't know what hell I've been through.' As she turned her head away from him, for fear she should betray herself, he touched her chin gently, making her look at him again. 'You wouldn't like to say whether you'd be willing to marry me or not, would you? Put me out of my misery—if it's possible?'

The last words, delivered in a hoarse voice, gave Kim some idea of the anguish which appeared to be eating him up. Not trying to hide what was in her eyes any longer, she lifted her arms to slide them slowly around his neck. 'I love you,' she said softly, 'I want to marry you more than anything in the world.'

With a smothered exclamation he began kissing her, then again visibly restrained himself. Laying her back on her pillows, he kissed her gently once more before drawing firmly away from her. 'Now that that's settled the rest might be a little easier, but we'll talk in the morning. Douglas prescribed some tablets to give you a good night's sleep, so while I still have some control left, you'd better take them.'

Kim remembered, next morning, trying to speak after doing as she was told, but Garrick wouldn't allow it, and she must have fallen asleep almost immediately. When she woke again she was drowsy, but there was none of the underlying apprehension she had known the night before.

Then she saw that Abby was sitting on a chair by her bed, where Garrick had been sitting. Garrick! Where was he? Panicking, she struggled to sit up, murmuring his name.

'Don't worry, he'll be here directly,' Abby hushed her with gentle sternness. 'He'd be here now if his mother and I hadn't managed to persuade him he'd be in no condition to do anything at all for his fiancée if he was falling asleep on his feet.'

'So—he told you?' Kim felt her cheeks colouring delicately as Abby smiled teasingly.

'I'm afraid I caught him putting the ring on your finger,' she confessed. 'I got quite a shock, I can tell you, until he explained how you'd been awake and agreed to marry him, and he wasn't going to give you a chance to change your mind. You could change the ring, he said, if you didn't like it, but that was all.'

'Oh, Abby!' Kim whispered, gazing at the beautiful sapphire ring which adorned the third finger of her left hand. 'I love him, and I'm so happy . . .'

Abby unashamedly brushed the tears from her eyes. 'Garrick's mother and I are happy too,' she smiled. 'Mrs Lang is sure there's no one she'd rather have for a daughter-in-law.'

'That's lovely of her,' Kim swallowed the lump in her throat with difficulty. 'I've been an awful nuisance!'

'No,' said Abby quickly, 'you haven't, but you lay there so quiet and still we wished you would be. Garrick was nearly demented—he refused to leave your side. Two nights he's never slept. I sent him off at five this morning, but I had to promise faithfully not to leave you and to call him at once when you woke.'

'What time is it now?' Kim couldn't believe he could care so much.

'Almost eight, lazybones,' Garrick's voice came teasing from the doorway. He was carrying a tray with two cups of tea. Coming into the room, he grinned at Abby. 'Something's wrong with my head this morning, I'm afraid. I forgot to bring a cup for you. The teapot's still full in the kitchen, though, and I know you'll be anxious to start breakfast.'

'Well, I'm not so old that I can't take a hint!' Abby jumped to her feet, looking amused. 'Don't tire Kim too much, though. I'll be back in half an hour.'

When Abby had gone, Garrick's face sobered as he closed the door firmly behind her. Returning to the bed, he sat down on it, very close. 'Are you still feeling better?' Again, as he had done so frequently the night before, his eyes searched her bruised face. 'That's one hell of a bump—and I want the truth!'

'My head's scarcely aching at all this morning,' she assured him. 'I really do feel fine.' As he looked less than impressed, she said hastily, 'How about you? Abby said you'd had no sleep.'

'Don't worry.' Bending forward suddenly, he kissed her swiftly, his eyes full of tenderness and smouldering desire. 'I'll make up for it between now and the wedding. I don't expect to sleep much afterwards,' he added wickedly.

As Kim coloured in adorable confusion, he took a cup of tea from the tray and, without waiting for her to speak, insisted she drank it. When she finished he gently touched the purple mark on her cheek.

'I suppose,' she sighed ruefully, 'I look a bit of a mess.'

'You'd be beautiful to me, whatever your face was like,' he growled. 'Don't you realise yet how much I love you?' Picking up her left hand, he kissed it softly. 'I left you this ring to remind you, if you woke up and I wasn't here. I don't know if you've really forgiven me?' His voice became strained while his face paled. 'Despite what I told Abby to the contrary, you have my full permission to change your mind. I just wanted you to be very sure of my intentions.'

Wondering if she should give in so easily, Kim tried to frown, but somehow found herself smiling instead, with her smiles turning to blushes as she exclaimed impulsively, 'I can see you're going to make a very remarkable husband!'

'So you didn't change your mind?'

Kim thought she had reassured him, but his expression was still grim, his eyes oddly tormented. 'Oh, darling!' she opened her arms to him, the pain she had suffered in the past fading before his obviously greater one, 'I've loved you almost since I first saw you. It wasn't just a fanciful crush. It was something which had never happened to me before, though, and it frightened me, to begin with. But I soon realised that loving you was as inescapable as the very air I breathed . . .'

She wasn't allowed any farther. With a low exclamation Garrick pulled her into his arms and for a while there was complete silence, broken only by his thick murmurings. Tenderly he kissed her lips and cheeks, touching the dark bruises almost reverently, his mouth a mixture of gentle compassion and restrained passion. As his hands grew bolder, seeking the lovely curves of her breasts, Kim began responding feverishly, feeling faint with the renewed and familiar urge to belong to him as she leant weakly against him. She recognised the hunger in his eyes and hands, just as she was aware of the control he was imposing on both their bodies as their lips clung and refused to part.

At last he drew away sharply. 'You tempt me until I can't think straight,' he said hoarsely.

'Does it matter?' she breathed, feeling herself trembling, wanting unashamedly to know his total possession.

With a severity only belied by the teasing glint in his eyes, he scolded sternly, 'Shameless hussy! Didn't you hear Abby say she'd be back directly with your breakfast? And before then I've a lot of explaining to do.'

'Does it matter?' Kim repeated, dazedly, suddenly uncaring of what was past as she thought of what the future held for her.

'Say that once again!' Garrick threatened.

Wryly Kim realised that while she would rather be back in his arms than listening to a lot of explanations which could probably wait, there were a few things she was curious about. 'Why did you go to see Joe, the day before yesterday?' she asked slowly.

Garrick replied grimly, never taking his eyes from her face, 'To tell him, and Rose too, of course, that I wanted to marry you.'

She stared at him amazed. 'When you believed I'd come expressly for that purpose!'

Bleakly his eyes darkened as he shook his head. 'I did, then suddenly I didn't any more. That was when I realised I couldn't trust a girl so completely and not love her. I'd actually loved you a long time,' he confessed, 'but refused to acknowledge it.'

For long seconds he stared at her, while they both remembered all the days and weeks of torment and misery. Thickly he said, 'I realised I loved you more than life itself, but everything had been against us from the beginning. You might understand if I tell you that over the years, my mother often tried to persuade Joe to invite Rose's relatives to visit, but he always swore that as they hadn't approved of him to start with he wasn't having them in his house. Then, apparently for no particular reason, he was all forgiveness, inviting you here, paying your fare, which was even more surprising as he rarely spends a penny on any one but himself. Even so, I wasn't really suspicious until he denied having your photograph, then after hearing him talking to you, that evening I took you home.'

'I wasn't listening properly to what he was saying,' Kim admitted, a shy confusion in her eyes while her cheeks flushed a delicate pink. 'You'd just kissed me and I think I was still slightly dazed. Did he imply that I was making a good job of leading you on or something?'

'Something like that,' he muttered absently, seeming suddenly more interested in the glowing loveliness of her face.

'I can see how you would be annoyed,' Kim whispered, 'but truly I had no idea.'

'I realise now,' Garrick said grimly, 'I didn't then, and I'm afraid I was becoming very sensitive where you were concerned. I was tempted to confront you, there and then, but although I'm ashamed to admit it, I was still curious to see how far you were prepared to go.'

'Why was Joe so against you marrying Irene Ross?' Kim frowned.

Garrick bent forward to kiss her softly, as if he must feel the softness of her mouth before he replied tersely. 'They've never got on. Since she was small, Irene's been coming to Coolarie, and the degree of antagonism between them had grown incredibly. Amazing really. Just one of those inexplicable things.'

'You don't like him much yourself, though?'

'No,' Garrick shook his head to Kim's rather timid query, 'but it's never been as bad as all that. Joe and I can work together after a fashion. Before my father died he asked me to keep Joe on. Once, when the plane my father was piloting crashed, Joe saved his life by pulling him out, but despite that, Joe has always maintained that his days here would be numbered if ever I married Irene. When she married someone else and went away, he visibly relaxed, but when she returned a widow, I think that was when he must have panicked and sent for you.' Smiling wryly, he added, 'That photograph your mother sent of her beautiful daughter must have been at least partly responsible for putting such a brilliant idea in his head!'

'I'm not so beautiful,' Kim protested anxiously.

'Yes, you are!' he retorted, so decisively that she dared not protest again. She felt quite bewildered by the things he was telling her and her wide-eyed gaze reflected her doubts clearly.

'It all seems so incredible!' she whispered.

Garrick shrugged ironically. 'As soon as I met you at the airport I understood his plan. If you married me his position on Coolarie would be quite safe. If it didn't work out then you might easily marry Brian and keep him near them for the rest of their lives.'

Kim's face paled; she felt completely stunned. Grasping Garrick's hand, in a frantic desire to convince him, she breathed, 'You must have known I wouldn't have come if I'd had even the slightest suspicion of that?'

'How could I be sure?' He raised the hand which so urgently clutched his to his lips. 'Anyway,' he grinned suddenly as she quivered at the touch of his mouth on her skin, 'I'm glad now you did—and that I decided, like a martyr, to play along.'

'You a martyr!' she tried to speak severely. 'More like a devil! You enjoyed leading me on!'

His smile widened, though his eyes pleaded forgiveness. 'I would never have believed I could succumb as easily to ordinary human weaknesses. Your blue eyes must have bewitched me, my darling. I was guilty of saying and doing a lot of things I normally wouldn't, just to entice you, I'm afraid. I do have other properties and go abroad occasionally, but my chief interest lies in the breeding of stud cattle, and I spent most of my days at Coolarie, doing just that.'

To share his life with him seemed to Kim a dazzling prospect, and she didn't try to hide the happiness in her eyes. Then her radiance faded with sudden remorse. 'In a way it must have been partly my fault that you thought I was in league with Uncle Joe. I was half in love with you almost at once and thought it silly to pretend otherwise.'

'The fault was chiefly mine,' Garrick said heavily. 'I'm used to Joe's senseless pranks, you aren't. I should have taken no notice. He has his good points, but he's not exactly the kind of man I usually take seriously. He spends all his money at race meetings. Not that I've anything against gambling in moderation, but Joe would willingly sell his soul for it. He's cashed about everything else, including his shares in the company.'

'He told me he never had any!'

'I'm not surprised.' Garrick's mouth tightened. 'He misleads people deliberately. I'm sorry to have to say this, Kim, but he's my relative as well.'

'What about Aunt Rose?' Kim asked anxiously.

'You mustn't blame her,' he said curtly, 'nor feel too sorry for her. She adores Joe—apparently just as he is. Or she's resigned to the fact that she can't change him. She may have had some vague idea as to what he had in mind, but you can be sure he wouldn't have told her much. He'd be too frightened she'd betray him. She has a lot more character in her little finger than Joe has in his whole body.'

Kim nodded, beginning to understand, but she couldn't help feeling a little apprehensive of the future, if Joe continued to be a thorn, so to speak, in Garrick's side. 'When are they coming home?' she asked nervously.

'Very soon, in time for our wedding.' Garrick's voice deepened. 'I'm not waiting, Kim. Just a few days, and if Joe can't make it, Rose will. He and Rose will be retiring to the coast after we return from our honeymoon. I'm busy buying them the house Rose liked. They're both delighted.'

It was almost too much to take in, and with Garrick regarding her with such an arrogant, determined glint in his eyes, how could she defy him? 'My parents?' she murmured weakly.

She might have known he would have taken care of that as well. 'I've been in touch,' he assured her gently. 'Like my mother, they're very happy for us and have no objection to an early marriage. I've promised you'll speak to them today, if you're well enough.'

Kim nodded eagerly, still slightly stunned, while her heart began beating wildly. In a short time she was to be Garrick's wife, living at Coolarie with him. 'They can visit us?' she pleaded.

'I've already asked them,' he smiled.

It seemed inevitable that the wonderful happiness that swept over her should be shadowed by one last flicker of doubt. 'What about Irene?' she whispered.

'What about her?' Garrick's dark brows rose cynically. 'She knows I never loved her. I'll admit I've taken her out occasionally to annoy Joe, but she's had affairs with more men than I'd care to count, both before and after her marriage. She's so tough, I don't think I could hurt her if I tried—although I felt like it,' he admitted grimly, his eyes smouldering, 'when she began ordering you around. Oh, my darling,' he groaned fiercely, 'I wanted to make you suffer, I did my best to, but when she started it was entirely different. I wanted to strike her!'

Kim's mind appeared to be swinging in disjointed circles. 'You would have let me go if Joe hadn't collapsed?'

'No!' He pulled her closer, his face white as he stared

at her, passion blazing from his eyes. 'You can believe, for all I said, nothing was farther from my mind. I was desperately trying to think of something which might keep you here and save my pride. What little I seemed to have left, anyway,' he finished dryly.

Kim's thoughts continued on a pendulum. 'The night of the barbecue, I was so unhappy.'

'You couldn't have known how I felt!' he muttered tersely. 'I wanted to make love to you—I almost did. It was only your innocence that stopped me.'

'Afterwards,' Kim swallowed, for even yet the pain she had suffered seemed fresh in her mind, 'afterwards you ignored me.'

'I attempted to,' he corrected grimly. 'I smiled at other women and all I saw was you. You were sitting under some trees and I couldn't recall feeling so bad in all my life. In the end I resorted, with the kind of desperation I've always despised, to drink, and even then I couldn't drown you out. I looked at you and realised how much I loved you—and felt as if I'd been hit by a bomb.'

'You didn't tell me?' she whispered, wide-eyed.

The hand he ran over her soft, fair hair shook slightly. 'I had to get rid of the Bronsons first, and Irene. I couldn't be sure how you felt about me. I was aware that the chemistry between us was right, but I wanted more than that. If you'd ever loved me, I feared I might have turned it to hate, and I didn't want anyone around while I found out. I wasn't sure how I would react if I'd lost you,' he paused and his voice roughened savagely. 'I don't want to remember how I felt when I thought I'd lost you for ever in that river!'

'Don't think of it any more,' she smiled tremulously. 'The river didn't get me, and you really saved my life by rescuing me as you did, because I could never have got home alone. I love you, and as long as you love me that's all that really matters.'

His arms tightened as he assured her thickly, 'I'm going to love you for the rest of your life.' His eyes smouldered with mounting passion as he kissed her mouth with a savage hunger. 'One day,' he muttered against her bruised lips, 'you might begin to realise how much you mean to me. Without you I'm nothing.'

'Darling,' her pulse raced in tune with his thundering heart, her voice little more than a ragged whisper, 'what we have seems almost too wonderful to be true. I can scarcely believe it.'

'Then I'll have to convince you,' he replied, with a hint of his old teasing arrogance. 'And I warn you, I'm going to be a very jealous husband. I won't allow you to so much as look at another man.'

'Do you think I'd ever want to?' she protested breathlessly, as he gathered her close again.

His face sobered abruptly. 'I love everything about you,' he murmured, kissing her with great tenderness. 'I love you so much I don't altogether trust myself.'

'Do you have to?' she whispered, surrendering to the feverish clamour of her blood and kissing him back. Blindly she pressed her lips to his strong brown throat, then more boldly against his mouth as she sensed his growing need.

'Wanton!' he muttered thickly, his mouth quirking but his eyes darkening with passion. 'I hope you realise exactly what you're inviting?'

As he bent over her, Kim nodded, seeing the love and desire in his eyes before her own closed with a rapturous quiver.

'Abby may be here in a minute!' she exclaimed suddenly, as, with a muffled groan, Garrick lifted her completely into his arms.

'Little coward!' His glance roamed the perfect shape of her, his eyes gently teasing again on her tremulous pink face. 'Did you hope to escape the consequences of your deliberate tantalising? Abby might be here in another minute, but we'll have every minute of our lives after that. Believe me, my darling, you won't ever get away.'

And she never did!

Harlequin Plus

A WORD ABOUT THE AUTHOR

Margaret Pargeter was born in the quiet Northumbrian Valley, in the extreme northeast of England, where she lives today.

When did she first feel an urge to write? "Truthfully, I can't recall," she admits. "It must have been during my early teens. I remember carrying a notebook in my pocket, and while milking cows I would often take a break to scribble something down."

The jottings developed into short stories, and Margaret's first break came several years after she had married. Her husband talked her into entering a writing contest, and her work caught the eye of an editor, who asked her to write serial stories. From there she went on to complete her first romance novel, *Winds from the Sea* (Romance #1899).

Among the author's many blessings, which she likes to keep counting, is the "pleasure I get from knowing that people enjoy reading my books. And," she adds, "I hope they long continue to do so."

ALL-TIME FAVORITE BESTSELLERS
...love stories that grow
more beautiful with time!

Now's your chance to discover the earlier great books in Harlequin Presents, the world's most popular romance-fiction series.

Choose from the following list.

ALL-TIME FAVORITE BESTSELLERS

Complete and mail this coupon today!

Harlequin Reader Service

In the U.S.A.
1440 South Priest Drive
Tempe, AZ 85281

In Canada
649 Ontario Street
Stratford, Ontario N5A 6W2

Please send me the following Presents **ALL-TIME FAVORITE
BESTSELLERS**. I am enclosing my check or money order
for $1.75 for each copy ordered, plus 75¢ to cover
postage and handling.

☐ #17	☐ #35	☐ #41	☐ #66	☐ #73
☐ #20	☐ #36	☐ #42	☐ #67	☐ #75
☐ #29	☐ #38	☐ #50	☐ #70	☐ #78
☐ #32	☐ #39	☐ #62	☐ #71	

Number of copies checked @ $1.75 each = $ _____
N.Y. and Ariz. residents add appropriate sales tax $ _____
Postage and handling $ ___.75___
TOTAL $ _____

I enclose _____·_____
(Please send check or money order. We cannot be
responsible for cash sent through the mail.)
Prices subject to change without notice.

NAME _____
(Please Print)

ADDRESS _____ APT. NO. _____

CITY _____

STATE/PROV. _____

ZIP/POSTAL CODE _____

Offer expires August 31, 1983   30556000000

Just what the woman on the go needs!

BOOK MATE

The perfect "mate" for all Harlequin paperbacks
Traveling • Vacationing • At Work • In Bed • Studying
• Cooking • Eating

Pages turn WITHOUT opening the strap.

Perfect size for all standard paperbacks, this wonderful invention makes reading a pure pleasure! Ingenious design holds paperback books OPEN and FLAT so even wind can't ruffle pages – leaves your hands free to do other things. Reinforced, wipe-clean vinyl-covered holder flexes to let you turn pages without undoing the strap...supports paperbacks so well, they have the strength of hardcovers!

SEE-THROUGH STRAP

Reinforced back stays flat.

Built in bookmark.

BOOK MARK

BACK COVER HOLDING STRIP

10" x 7¼", opened.
Snaps closed for easy carrying, too.

Available now. Send your name, address, and zip or postal code, along with a check or money order for just $4.99 + .75 ¢ for postage & handling (for a total of $5.74) payable to Harlequin Reader Service to:

Harlequin Reader Service

In U.S.
P.O. Box 22188
Tempe, AZ 85282

In Canada
649 Ontario Street
Stratford, Ont. N5A 6W2

Introducing...

Harlequin American Romance

An exciting new series of sensuous and emotional love stories—contemporary, engrossing and uniquely American. Long, satisfying novels of conflict and challenge, stories of modern men and women dealing with life and love in today's changing world.

7003

Available now wherever paperback books are sold, or through Harlequin Reader Service:

In the U.S.
1440 South Priest Drive
Tempe, AZ 85281

In Canada
649 Ontario Street
Stratford, Ontario N5A 6W2

"Falling in love happens to us all."

Kim had forgotten her mother's words until she met handsome rancher Garrick Lang. No one before him had ever left her breathless, imagining pleasures yet to be discovered.

It seemed fate had prompted Kim's uncle to send her an airline ticket and an invitation to spend six months in Australia. For if he hadn't done so, she might never have met the man she now loved so completely.

Innocent herself, how could Kim suspect there was a darker purpose to her relative's gift—and her lover's passion?

MARGARET PARGETER began writing short stories in her teens and later wrote serials for a newspaper. Since her first romantic novel, she has been delighting readers everywhere.

The most popular romance fiction all over the world...

Harlequin Books

...because no one touches the heart of a woman quite like Harlequin!

Internet Archive
Man from the Kimberleys
ISBN: 0373105959
UsedGood

2012-11-14
E1283C3
2

373-10595-9

65373 00

PRINTED IN U.S.A.